Miss D'Amico put out her cigarette, though she hadn't smoked half of it. Her mouth curled in a small, polite yawn. "I'm sorry," she said. "It's been a long day for me. I didn't sleep well last night."

Nor will you sleep well tonight, I was tempted to say.

I had come to tell her the servants' gossip, that behind the gray stone wall she found so ugly, there lay two bodies—the body of my mother and the body of a man, her lover.

Also by Scott O'Dell:

ISLAND OF THE BLUE DOLPHIN
BLACK PEARL
KING'S FIFTH
DARK CANOE
SING DOWN THE MOON
THE CRUISE OF THE ARCTIC STAR
CHILD OF FIRE
THE TWO-HUNDRED NINETY
ZIA
CARLOTA
KATHLEEN, PLEASE COME HOME
THE CAPTIVE
SARAH BISHOP
THE FEATHERED SERPENT
THE AMETHYST RING
THE CASTLE IN THE SEA*
ALEXANDRA*
THE ROAD TO DAMIETTA*
STREAMS TO THE RIVER, RIVER TO THE SEA*
BLACK STAR, BRIGHT DAWN*

*Published by Fawcett Books

THE SPANISH SMILE

Scott O'Dell

FAWCETT JUNIPER • NEW YORK

Contents

1 The Steel Bracelet   1
2 The Smile of Teresa Benivides   10
3 Ramón's Revenge   20
4 The Gray Stone Wall   24
5 Jennifer's Mistake   37
6 Visions   45
7 Escape   51
8 Farewell to Freedom   56
9 Santiago, the Mad Dream   61
10 The Intruder   73
11 The Crystal Caskets   81
12 Fatal Words   86
13 The Nineteenth   95
14 Eve's Friend, the Serpent   105
15 Visitors from the Mainland   110
16 Guardian of the Gate   119
17 Cu, Cu, Curu, Paloma   127
18 The Wolfes   132
19 Behind the Wall   139
20 Journey to a Strange Land   143

Out of reality are our tales of imagination fashioned.

—HANS CHRISTIAN ANDERSEN

1

The Steel Bracelet

There was no lighthouse on Isla del Oro, although two ships had gone around there in the past year and five in my memory. The nearest light stood at Point Firmin, across the channel thirty miles away. On clear nights I could see it from my tower, shining red and then green and then red again.

In place of a lighthouse there were two whistling buoys, one in the shallows at the northernmost point of the island and one to the south where the water was deep. On calm days they made sounds no louder than a curlew's cry, but during a storm, when the gray-black waves came down from Alaska, they moaned and between the moans there were long, drawn-out sighs, as if the land and the sea and the world itself were in mortal pain.

The ship that went aground on Isla del Oro last December, less than a month ago, came from Panama with a cargo of animals and reptiles for the San Francisco zoo. She struck the southern reef in a heavy fog and broke up, spilling some of her cargo on the beach. All of the animals were rescued, except a quetzal bird, three rare monkeys, and a pair of bushmasters. The monkeys were found later, but the quetzal bird and the two serpents were still roaming around somewhere.

My father, Don Enrique de Cabrillo y Benivides, received a letter just this week from the curator of the zoo describing the quetzal bird and the bushmaster snakes.

"The quetzal, *Pharomachrus mocinna*," he wrote, "is golden-green with scarlet, iridescent plummage and a long, flowing upper tail covert. Prized and worshipped by the ancient Maya Indians, it is a bird of surpassing beauty, extremely rare, and very secret in its habits. Its call is a single, melodious note not unlike that of a thrush."

The curator went on to describe the serpents, which he seemed to value less than the quetzal bird. "The bushmaster, *Lachesis muta*," he wrote, "is a pit viper more than twelve feet in length, marked by black bars and pink shading. Its aggressive nature, its ability, because of its length, to strike human prey in the throat, and its long fangs supplied with copious venom, make the bushmaster the deadliest snake in the world, deadlier than the king cobra or the mamba. Extreme care in handling the bushmaster is suggested. It may be well to remember, however, that this viper is reluctant to attack unless provoked."

Captain Vega and his *pistoleros,* who guard our island night and day, have been given descriptions of the bird and the serpents with instructions to capture the one and kill the others. So far they have not been successful, though they have brought in, as proof of their diligence, three of the large but harmless snakes that inhabit Isla del Oro.

Perhaps I should explain a little about Isla del Oro. In 1542, when my ancestor Juan Rodriguez Cabrillo sighted the island, he thought it was two islands, not one, and named it after his caravels, *La Victoria* and *San Salvador.* Nearly a hundred years later another explorer, Sebastián Vizcaíno, sailed by and gave the island a different name. It was my grandfather who, after he discovered gold on the island, gave it still another name, Isla del Oro. That was after the days when Spain owned all the land from Alaska to Peru, including California, Baja and Alta both.

It had been storming for a week, with heavy winds lashing the castle walls and great waves driving down from the Aleutians. You could see the waves looming far away on the horizon. At first they looked like hills, low gray hills on the moon or on a moonlit desert. As they drew near they changed their shape but not their color, and looked like a herd of prehistoric beasts as they stampeded headlong against the island, one after the other.

The walls of my tower, like the walls all through the castle, measured more than four feet in thickness, made of hard blue and white stones hewn from the living ledges of our gold mines. Yet they trembled as waves crashed against the island.

Storms in January usually lasted a week or more, which meant that my plans for the next day—my sixteenth birthday—were very much in doubt. Our ship the *Infanta,* was big and seaworthy, but with me, his only child, on board would my father allow her to cross the channel in such heavy weather?

I have been on the mainland only once in my lifetime. It was on my ninth birthday, when I went to visit my grandmother, Doña Gertrudis. I was only there from one morning to the next, yet remembering this time it seems more like a month. So many things happened to me that never happened before . . .

On the wharf that morning, as the *Infanta* strained at her moorings and pearly smoke drifted from her stack, Don Enrique's cold hands slipped a bracelet on my wrist. It had two parts that snapped shut like tiny jaws, and was fastened by a chain to a bracelet worn by my nurse, Prudencia.

I glanced at the bracelet in childish wonder. I lifted my arm to examine it and felt a sharp jerk as Prudencia resisted this movement. My wonder changed to surprise, then to dismay.

"Never fear," my father said, taking a key from his pocket. "Tomorrow, the moment you step from the ship, I'll unlock you."

"But why do you lock me now?" Once when I was three my nurse had tied me to a bedpost for being unruly. "What have I done to displease you?"

"Nothing, my dear Lucinda. It is for your safety, these precautions. You are visiting a country of barbarians. Go with God and without danger. But give strict attention to your nurse, who is a woman of good sense. As for your grandmother, do not mind what she says. She is very old and full of fancies. When she was younger she also had fancies. They are stranger now."

He sent *pistoleros* with us, two tall Yaqui Indians with knives strapped to their thighs and Skorpion pistols in their concha belts.

Prudencia was stout as an oak stump. We went up the gangplank side by side, one half-step apart. The handcuffs and the links that joined them looked fragile but they were made of the hardest steel. Our bones would break, hers and mine, before the chains would ever fail. The *pistoleros,* two unsmiling shadows, watched us from under their wide-brimmed hats.

My grandmother's ranch stretched for miles along the Mexican border east of San Diego. It once covered twenty-one thousand acres, but in 1855 her grandfather, Pancho de Benivides, traded two thousand acres for a black horse and a pair of white gloves.

In the early days it was known by the name *El Rancho de los Dos Hermanos,* Ranch of the Two Brothers. It was later called *Rancho Santa Gertrudis,* after my grandmother. She raised cattle. When the pastures dried up in late summer, half of her herds were shipped to Isla del Oro aboard the *Infanta* and turned out to graze in our canyons. My father had nothing to do with this operation. In fact, he disliked cattle and tolerated them only because Doña Gertrudis threatened to strike him from her will and leave the ranch to the nuns of Mount Olive.

Prudencia and I, trailed by the two *pistoleros,* arrived at Santa Gertrudis near sundown after a three-hour voyage and a dusty trip by automobile. There were musicians at the gate playing "El Rancho Grande" to enliven our spritis and pitchers of pink lemonade to quench our thirst. But I was not enlivened, as I remember. Every link of the chain that bound me to Prudencia seemed made of lead.

Shaking in my shoes, I was led into a vaulted room lit by candles like a church. At the far end of the room I saw the dim figure of my grandmother, sitting on what I thought was a throne trimmed in velvet, swathed in a cloud of lavender silk. Her feet were clad in golden slippers and rested upon the back of an Indian boy who, crouched upon his hands and knees, served her as a footstool.

Not until I was very close did I see that she was seated not upon a throne, but upon a nest of pink cushions in a high-backed chair on wheels. Her forehead was long and narrow and she had, I remember, a long, thin nose, straight as a stiletto. Except for her braided hair, she could have been my father, Don Enrique, looking down at me.

She held out a withered hand that was cold like his.

Clutching at the chain that bound my wrist, trying to hide it from her gaze, I kissed her knuckles with trembling lips. Our eyes met. There was a short silence. Then my grandmother gasped and leaned forward from her wheelchair to get a better view of me. I lowered my eyes in embarrassment.

"Look up," she said. "Raise your pretty head."

I glanced at the candles burning above her, at her feet resting on the back of the Indian boy, at my nurse.

"Look at me," she cried. "At me, child!"

It was hard to do. She reached out and lifted my chin, grasping it tight in her dry fingers until finally I looked at her. We stared at each other.

"Holy Mother," she muttered to herself, not once but

twice. Then she said, "Teresa! It is Teresa de Cabrillo y Benivides who stands here."

I had never heard the name before.

"Teresa is your grandmother seven times removed," Doña Gertrudis explained. "Alas, her life was tragic from the moment of her birth. In the black plague that swept Spain—she was only five—Teresa lost her mother and father. She survived the sickness but it left her with a weakened heart in a frail body. She was very talented. She was even considered a prodigy on the harpsichord. Imagine—a prodigy!"

Doña Gertrudis must have seen something in my face that made her pause. She took a sip of a cloudy drink that a servant offered her.

"A girl of talent," she said. "A tragic life. It brings tears to my eyes when I think of it."

A small tear did well up beneath one of her lids. Her bony fingers still held my chin. She thrust her face toward me. A round, black mole at the corner of her mouth glistened.

"Light!" she cried. "I need light." At once a servant appeared with a sconce of burning candles. "Shine them upon the darling's face," my grandmother directed. "Closer, closer. That's it. Yes, it is Teresa," she said and was silent again.

"What happened to her? What? Tell me."

"Holy Mercy! By evil chance she encountered Murillo, the great painter, at a reception given by the King. He was fascinated with her. With her smile. And painted her portrait, taking pains and time. That was the last she ever saw of him. But Teresa had fallen in love with the famous man. She wrote him letters that she never mailed. She composed poems about him that she tore up. She languished and died for love of him."

My grandmother gave a long sigh or resignation. "Take the light away," she said. "I can see. I am not blind. You have noticed Teresa's portrait, the one that Murillo painted? It hangs in the music room on Isla del Oro. No? Well, you are a bit young to notice such things. I gave it to your father when he married your mother, God rest her soul. I regret that I did. It is worth a fortune, and he has never liked it. A fortune!''

Doña Gertrudis glanced around into the shadowy corners of the room, at a figure of the Virgin. Then she flung her arms about my shoulders, as if to protect me from all mischance, from the turns and twistings of fate, from unrequited love, from farewells said too soon or too late, from the sharp teeth of time.

Suddenly she drew back. ''What is this?'' she snorted.

Her hand had become entangled in the steel chain. It was pulling the three of us together, clumsily holding us fast.

''You are chained!'' Doña Gertrudis said, extricating herself. ''Why? Who did this? A child in chains—who thought of such a barbarous thing? Your father?''

I was silent, ashamed to answer.

''Don Enrique, of course,'' she said. ''Does he think that I will steal you? Perhaps I shall.''

The chain tightened on my wrist. Prudencia untangled us and drew me closer.

''Did he fasten the chain on you when your mother fled? Since that night have you worn it?''

''Only today,'' I said.

''A disgrace even for a day. And Don Enrique will answer for it. Perhaps not to me, the woman who gave him birth, who foolishly gave him the fabulous island of gold. No, not to me, but certainly to God.''

Doña Gertrudis was out of breath. Servants brought fans and fanned her. She was silent for a long time. I thought she had gone to sleep when she abruptly sat up ans smiled at me.

''Did you bring clothes with you?'' she said.

''No, Grandmother. Don Enrique has let me come only for today. The next time I will bring them.''

''You are a child, Lucinda, and you have no one to

7

play with on the island. You can't play with the Indian children, surely.''

"I am not allowed to play with them.''

"What do you do? You have tutors. You have learned French and English. You speak the purest of Castilian. You study, I know, but . . .''

"I read. I read a book every day.''

"What books?''

"Dickens, sometimes. And Sir Walter Scott. Now I am reading *Don Quixote.* ''

"You don't have to read about Don Quixote. You have a Don Quixote living on Isla del Oro.''

"What do you mean?''

"Your father. But not a gentle Don Quixote. An arrogant, evil one.'' She took a sip of her cloudy drink.

"Come, my darling, and live with me. I will talk to Don Enrique. I will write to him tomorrow.''

I *was* lonely on Isla del Oro and often fearful of my father. But Doña Gertrudis, sitting in her wheelchair among mountains of lavender pillows in a strange room full of shadows and the smell of incense, repelled me.

"But now we shall have fun,'' she said and ordered the musicians to play, the servants to bring cookies and cake. And when I left that night, suffering a stomach ache, she gave me a satin box marked "Too short to tie,'' stuffed with pieces of colored ribbons.

"When you come to live with me,'' she said, "I will have another pretty box for you.''

I never saw Doña Gertrudis again. She died a few months later, willing her nineteen-thousand-acre ranch and everything she owned to the sisters of Mount Olive.

I opened the window, the only one in my tower. It was small and barred—more like the opening in a prison wall than a window. Now and then a half moon showed among driving clouds. The monstrous waves from the north were breaking against the shore. Across the channel between rifts in the heavens, I saw warning flashes of red and green. The storm would last for two more days, at least.

Already late for dinner, I closed the window and hurried along the marble staircase that wound down and down, floor after floor, in a dizzy spiral.

2

The Smile of
Teresa Benivides

At Don Enrique's request I went downstairs each night an hour before he appeared, either to the small dining room if we were eating alone, or to the large one if we were entertaining guests.

My task was to arrange the flowers, to see that they were fresh, with preference given to shades of red, and carefully to pour a long-stemmed crystal glass two-thirds full of La Ina and put it beside his plate, so the sherry would be precisely at room temperature when he sat down.

To make certain that the wine would be to his liking I had to sample a drop or two. La Ina is a parched wine, so dry that it puckers the mouth. I didn't care for this task. Especially since there was always a butler at hand who was a better wine-taster than me. But I never said so, and faithfully went through the ceremony each night. It was a penance my father had imposed upon me for being the descendant of conquistadors and the only daughter of one of the richest men in God's rich kingdom.

Jennifer Delaney was standing at the table when I walked

into the dining room. Jennifer was the latest woman to appear on the island. In the eight years since my mother left there had been more than a dozen *gringas* on Isla del Oro.

Jennifer was a few years older than I, tall and slender with frizzed hair that stood up around her head like a ragged halo. Ten days ago, when she stepped off the *Infanta* dressed in tangerine silk and tangerine shoes that were so airy I wondered how they stayed on her feet, I thought she was the prettiest *gringa* I had ever seen.

Jennifer also had a daily task. In the morning she went to the kitchen and took down the menu the chef had selected for dinner that night. (Don Enrique liked to be surprised, so the menu was never routine—poached salmon with eels vinaigrette on Fridays, rack of lamb on Saturdays, and so forth. Always there were three entrées to choose from, with wonderful vegetables that came from our gardens. The desserts were always architecturally inventive.)

"Do we have guests for dinner?" I asked Jennifer.

"No, just the regulars—Captain Wolfe and his wife. Father Martínez. The headman of the *pistoleros*—I never can remember his name . . ."

"Vega."

"Captain Vega and his wife. That's all."

"Is there any news?" I asked the same question every night. "This is Saturday. Something must have happened."

"A miner's wife down in the village gave birth to triplets. All of them are healthy."

There was no radio, no television on Isla del Oro. No magazines came to the island. No newspapers. Although the mainland was only a few miles away, we might have been living on another planet. Happenings at the mines—accidents, the amount of ore brought to the smelter, the number of gold bars shipped away, the price of gold on the world market—these things were recounted. Servants invented rumors and passed them around. I invented a few myself. This was the news that circulated on the island.

"There's something else," Jennifer said. "Captain Vega found a character digging on the south beach this morning."

From time to time the unwary ventured onto Isla del Oro. If they came by boat they were promptly run off. If they were put ashore by confederates who then disappeared, they were roundeed up by our *pistoleros* and hustled back to the mainland. Once a helicopter had landed. Most were prospectors who had heard of the famous Isla del Oro mines and hoped to pick up a fortune in nuggets before they were discovered.

"A prospector," I said.

"No, he had a sack filled with bones when the *pistoleros* arrested him."

"Then he's an anthropologist. Captain Vega found one last summer digging around in the same location."

"He's in the guardhouse now," Jennifer said. "Your father has been down there all afternoon talking to him."

"Strange," I said. "That last one was here on the island for only an hour after he was arrested."

"Strange?" Jennifer said. "*Everything* on the island is strange."

I said nothing.

Jennifer lowered her voice. "Even your father is strange. I don't understand him."

"You are new here in Castillo Santiago," I said. "Don Enrique's strangeness is something to keep to yourself. I advise you not to think about it, and if you do, to keep your thoughts to yourself."

"You're angry with me?" Jennifer said.

"No, I am your friend. A friend who can give you a warning, I hope."

She finished the place cards and left without another word.

Jennifer ate with the servants. In a month or two, if she were on the island that long, Don Enrique would invite her to eat with us, as he had the other *gringas*. He admired her artistry with cards, the way she fashioned the letters so they looked like the lettering in an old manuscript, as if a patient nun had made them. She had learned the art by herself, after she received a calligraphy set for Christmas.

My father was smiling when he sat down to dinner. He laid aside the book he had brought to the table, selected the food he wished to eat, took a sip of wine, and glanced at me in approval. His two big staghounds arranged themselves on either side of him.

Don Enrique was tall and very thin and carried himself stiffly as if he had a sword thrust down his back. He wore a trim beard that came to a point and curled out a little at the end. His hands were long-fingered and pale and on his right thumb he had an intaglio ring of black onyx made in the sixteenth century by the master craftsman Benvenuto Cellini.

Tonight he was dressed in the black doublet and long silk hose of a courtier during the reign of King Carlos the Second. In his vast clothes press he had dozens of costumes of that peroid, which he wore to suit the occasion.

"You made a good catch this morning," he said, raising his glass to Captain Vega, who sat across the table from him. "Even though one of your men became overzealous and almost finished off Señor Dawson. I talked to him for a while this afternoon and found him a little hazy. But he will come around in a day or two, I trust. What do you think, Doctor Wolfe?"

"The young man is much better tonight," Doctor Wolfe said. "I saw him just before we cane here. He should be up and around within a week. Or less."

Gerda Wolfe was the surgeon in charge of our hospital. She had a long neck and a round head that looked small because she wore her hair cut tight to her skull.

Don Enrique turned to Father Martínez, a thin little man huddled in a rusty cloak. "I have been thinking about a plan," he said. "I have been thinking about it for a long time now. I wonder if you will approve."

Father Martínez was accustomed to my father's plans. He

knew that whether he approved the plan or not, it would make little difference. He put down his fork and listened.

"You will recall," Don Enrique said, "that I have an ancestor named Juan Rodriguez Cabrillo. You will also recall that he died on nearby San Miguel, and is buried there."

Father Martínez nodded, darted a glance at the crisp slice of abalone waiting on his plate, and said that he remembered well.

"Cabrillo has been there for centuries," he said. "May God rest his soul."

"It is my wish," Don Enrique went on, "to remove Admiral Cabrillo from that alien place. To bring him here to Isla del Oro."

Father Martínez, startled by the idea, made the sign of the cross, touching his bony forehead and his high thin shoulders. As for myself, I had known about the idea for years and about the details of Juan Cabrillo's death.

After he discovered Isla del Oro, Admiral Cabrillo had sailed north along the coast of California and had rounded Point Conception, a few leagues beyond Santa Barbara, when his caravels were struck by a violent storm that drove them south to the shores of San Miguel.

There, while seeing to the repairs on the ships, he fell and broke his arm.

Cabrillo insisted upon continuing his voyage, but blood poisoning set in when he had traveled a few leagues north of San Francisco, and he was forced to abandon the voyage.

He turned back to the haven of San Miguel. After a few days of delirium he died.

On the day that the crypt deep beneath the castle was finished, Don Enrique began to dream about moving the admiral's remains from San Miguel to Isla del Oro.

Father Martínez, having recovered from his astonishment, said, "I foresee difficulties in finding the grave and . . ."

"It is not the difficulties that concern me," Don Enrique

said. "Is it proper, I ask you, to disturb the grave? Is it an unchristian act?"

"There are cases where this has been done," Father Martínez replied. "The great Raimundo Lull, killed by the heathen Moors and buried in Africa, was removed therefrom and returned to his native Spain."

"A worthy precedent," Don Enrique said. "There are others that I would like to bring here and will do so. Portolá, for one. Father Serra by all means, perhaps Francisco Pizarro."

"Pizarro would present difficulties. He is buried in Peru, I believe. In Lima."

"Not buried, Father. I have seen him. He lies on display for tourists to gawk at. In the Cathedral, all hunched up in a crystal box not big enough for a child. He looks like a monkey lying there. This is how the conqueror of the southern continent is treated. Shameful! I shall give him a decent burial on Isla del Oro and a spacious tomb to match his spacious mind and victories."

"He couldn't read or write his name, I have heard."

"Still, his mind was spacious," Don Enrique said. "He dreamed a large dream and achieved it."

"By promising freedom to the Emperor Atahualpa if only he would fill a vast room with gold. Then, the room filled to overflowing, Pizarro went back on his word and had the Inca murdered."

"You think this treachery, Father? If Pizarro had not done away with the Inca he would have done away with himself. Remember that he and his small band were surrounded by thousands of the enemy, bent upon their destruction."

"I would respect him more had he killed the Inca outright and not broken his solemn word."

"You will be uncomfortable if I bring him here? You won't say a prayer in his behalf?"

"A long prayer," Father Martínez said. "Very long."

Cutting the abalone on his plate into two equal pieces, my

father gave one to each of the staghounds and turned to Captain Wolfe.

"Are you familiar with San Miguel?" he asked the captain.

"I have passed it but never anchored," Captain Wolfe said. He was a lean, handsome man with wavy hair turning gray. "I don't have a chart of San Miguel, but I can get one."

"It turns out," Don Enrique said, "that the young man Vega almost killed is an anthropologist and has dug for fossils on the island. He dug there just before he came to Isla del Oro."

They went on talking about the expedition. I didn't listen. Tomorrow was my birthday, and for a special gift my father had promised that I could visit the mainland. He had made this promise every year on my birthday since the winter I went to visit Doña Gertrudis.

I waited. The conversation finally ended. My father picked up the book he had brought to the table and began to read. He always read when he wasn't talking or when the table talk bored him, holding his place with one finger while he ate.

Tonight, from glimpses I caught of pages peppered with dialogue, he was reading a story. For months now the books he brought to the table concerned Damascus steel. Alexander the Great had carried weapons of this metal, which came from India and was made into swords by European craftsmen.

The secret of making Damascus steel, known for its exceptional toughness and its quality of keeping a sharp cutting edge, was lost sometime after the Middle Ages. My father, who owned dozens of the swords, thought he might discover the secret again, and went to a laboratory he had at the smelter. He worked there every afternoon, experimenting with common steel, mixing it with gold and silver and even diamonds.

So far without success. The glowing steel shattered when it was quenched in water. In the days of Alexander, he told me, it was quenched by plunging the red-hot blade into the belly of a fat Nubian slave. He regretted that we had many fat bellies on Isla del Oro, but no Nubians. He was serious about this.

"What is the book?" I said, getting ready to ask about my birthday gift.

"A detective story. *Un Modelo para la Muerte.*"

"I have never heard of it."

"You have heard of Borges. He should have won the Nobel Prize long ago."

Don Enrique knew very well that I hadn't heard of Borges, for he had forbidden me to read books written in the twentieth century. He encouraged me to read. His library was always open. But only for authors who lived and wrote before the year 1900—that was the year the world started to fall apart, he said.

"*A Model for Death* is one of his first books," my father said. "A collaboration between him and a writer called Casares. They wrote it under the pseudonym of B. Suarez Lynch."

"It's exciting?"

"No. Dull. Few signs of the great writer to be. It will encourage you in your writing to know that the great Borges cathedral began with one small stone."

"In my case, a pebble."

"A handful, my dear Lucinda."

It was the first time he had ever encouraged me about my writing, though he had looked at two of the poems I had composed and returned them without comment.

"Tell me," he said, "what would you like for your birthday? It is tomorrow, you know."

"Have you forgotten your promise? That I could go to the mainland. To Los Angeles. Perhaps to Santa Barbara. To the ranch Ramón de Benivides once owned."

"The *Infanta* in this weather would be dangerous. At least very uncomfortable. Is there something nice, Lucinda, that you would like? You are too young for a diamond. A nice string of pearls. With an emerald clasp. Would that please you?"

17

"I have a string of pearls," I said. "The ones that belonged to Mother."

It was a spiteful thing to say.

My father's gaunt face darkened. His gaze sought me out. For a moment I imagined him as the Grand Inquisitor sitting in the courtyard of the Alcazar in Seville, watching, his small, sharp eyes hidden far in his head, watching while I was led out to be fed to the flames.

"Captain Wolfe," I said, raising my voice so my father could not help but hear me. "Can the *Infanta* make a crossing tomorrow? Don Enrique says it's too stormy."

Captain Wolfe hesitated, glanced at my father, then back at me. "Stormy, yes, Lucinda, but that aside, the ship's engines are being overhauled. She won't be ready, unfortunately, for another week."

Don Enrique went on reading and let the moment pass. He knew that I'd trapped him in a lie, that I knew he'd never had any thought of allowing me to visit the mainland.

At the close of dinner I excused myself and went to the music room, leaving the rest to talk about the removal of Juan Rodriguez Cabrillo from San Miguel. A mad scheme, the latest of several that Don Enrique had undertaken in the recent past—since the night my mother, Francesca, fled the island.

The music room had been designed for concerts—a parquet floor, walls covered with purple damask and dotted with sunburst mirrors—but at the far end was a small, paneled alcove that looked out upon the sea. It was here I kept a store of music and my harpsichord.

The harpsichord was a beautiful instrument, its frame made of fruitwood inlaid with enameled flowers—Rameau, the French composer, had once used it. I always enjoyed the hours spent here, but on this night my fingers felt clumsy. I played a few notes and stopped.

Above the harpsichord hung the portrait of my ancestress, Teresa de Cabrillo y Benivides.

Against a background of red velvet curtains Murillo's

18

portrait shows a girl seated at a harpsichord much as I was. Her fingers are on the keys, but she is looking directly out of the canvas at some intruder who has surprised her in the act of playing.

Murillo called his painting *The Spanish Smile*. I first examined it years before, the night I returned from my visit with Doña Gertrudis. I was attracted by the girl's white dress against the scarlet background. It was only later that I sought out the feature that gave the portrait its name.

In shadow, in Murillo's deepest blending of silver and black, the mouth is almost hidden. Unless you see the portrait at night, when candles illumine it from both sides at once, it's the girl's eyes that catch your attention. They are the color of silver.

Silver has many hues. It is the underside of a dove's wing, of mist as the sun is rising. It can be tinged with pigments from white to black. Teresa's eyes are the color of silver as it comes pure from the furnace, tinged with the faintest hint of blue.

But though the eyes are a part of the smile, it is the mouth that gives the portrait its name. I had often tried to describe it to myself and always failed. Not until I read about the young princess Lisa Bolkónskaya in *War and Peace* was I satisfied that I saw how the smile was composed.

"Her pretty little upper lip," Tolstoi wrote, "on which a delicate dark brown was just perceptible, was too short for her teeth, but it lifted all the more sweetly and was especially charming when she occasionally drew it down to meet the lower lip."

Yes, this defect was the source of Teresa's smile. And of mine. And yet there was something else to the smile that Murillo painted. Around the parted lips there hovered the shadow of unspoken words. It was something that Teresa was about to say to the intruder, perhaps the man she loved, that now, after centuries had passed, she was trying to say to me.

3

Ramón's Revenge

The young man Captain Vega had discovered digging on the beach and had struck on the head recovered in less than a month, though there were days during this time that he came close to death.

When he was on his feet again and could think straight, Don Enrique gave him a choice. He could return safely to the mainland or undertake the delicate, perhaps dangerous, work of removing Admiral Cabrillo's remains from San Miguel. The young man—his name was Christopher Dawson—apparently did not hesitate. He was studying at some university on the mainland and the Cabrillo project fitted nicely into his work.

All of this I knew only from hearsay. My father told me nothing about his agreement with Mr. Dawson and I didn't meet him until the night before the *Infanta* sailed.

The winter storms had ended, but it had been raining now for days, a gentle *chubasco* that blew in from the southeast and Mexico. I was on the terrace, saying goodbye to Father Martínez who was on his way to conduct mass in the village.

Justino, the lamplighter, had just begun to move along the driveway with his torch when a carriage drew up and a man stepped out. Through a tunnel of light in the falling rain he came toward me, walking slowly, a deliberate stride at a time. He was very tall, or seemed so. His hair fell long to his shoulders and shone dark in the rain and lantern light.

That afternoon I had been reading *Wuthering Heights*— for the third time in the past year, the fifth time since I was twelve. I was living with Emily Brontë and her people on the misty moors of England, not on Isla del Oro. And striding toward me was not Christopher Dawson, the anthropologist, but Heathcliff himself, pale of face but happy, appearing out of the stormy night to greet Cathy Earnshaw.

Mr. Dawson spoke my name—he must have—in the soft yet anguished tones that Heathcliff used with Cathy. And the magic lasted. Through the dinner, in the glow of the candles and the shadowy reflections cast by mirrors, it was Heathcliff I saw—at those rare moments when I dared to glance in his direction. It lasted through the night in my dreams and when I was awake and early the next morning as we sailed through the Narrows and headed north into the open sea.

Before we left the harbor my father reminded me that I was not invited on the voyage either to entertain Mr. Dawson or to be entertained by him. Indeed, he ordered me to remember that for all of his intelligence and efforts to be friendly, the anthropologist was still a *gringo*.

There were several reasons why I was on board the *Infanta*. For one thing, my father had suffered a prick of conscience at having refused my birthday wish. For another, as things turned out, he wished to embarrass Mr. Dawson. He also wished to show me in a quiet way just how thoroughly the *gringo* had destroyed the land our ancestors had discovered.

"This island we are leaving," he said to Mr. Dawson while Castillo Santiago still loomed high above us, "was a grant to my great-great-great-grandfather Gaspar de Beni-

vides. It was given to him by the King of Spain for ser-
vices in behalf of the crown. His son Ramón landed at the
port of Vera Cruz in Mexico and started off over the mountains for California. After a *jornada* of one hundred and
sixty-nine days through jungle and desert, on foot much of
the journey, he reached the *pueblo* of Los Angeles. That
was in 1821.''

The two men were standing on the foredeck, Don Enrique
wrapped in a heavy yellow slicker, Mr. Dawson in Levi's
and a checkered shirt, his head bare to the rain and his long
hair flying. I stood some distance away, but my father had
raised his voice; he was speaking to me rather than to Mr.
Dawson.

He pointed eastward to where the light on Point Firmin
flashed red and green, toward the city that lay beyond it.

''The *pueblo* is now a metropolis,'' he said, ''but you
won't see much of it because it's hidden behind a curtain of
smog, a curtain so dirty that even the rain can't wash it
away.''

He went on with Ramón's story, turning now and again to
face me, to make certain that I was listening. I had heard the
story before many times, both from him and from my
mother. I knew it by heart—how Ramón de Benivides had
gone on to Santa Barbara, settled down on his ranch, and
married the prettiest girl in the village.

A part of the grant was Isla del Oro, known then as Isla
Encantada, but Ramón never went out to the island. He was
on his way there when the war between Mexico and the
United States broke out. Instead, he rode south and joined a
bank of *guerrilleros* who were getting ready to defend their
ranches and their lives against the *gringos*.

A stiff wind was whipping the sea, sending spray over the
bow. Don Enrique faced me, having reached the place in his
story where the *gringo* army came marching into California
along the Mexican border, bent upon capturing San Diego.

''*Hola!*'' he cried out above the sound of the wind and the
pounding sea. ''*Hola!* But the Spaniards surprised them in

the valley of San Pascual. The army numbered more than a hundred, the *rancheros* less than twenty, but they were the best horsemen in the world. They rode swiftly out of the mist, shouting "Santiago and at them!"

This had been the rallying cry of Spaniards since the day they drove the infidel Moors from the soil of Spain. Don Enrique shouted it again, his voice rising to a scream. "Santiago and at them!"

He lowered his voice. "The Spaniards were armed only with lances made of river willows and tipped with iron files. Yet in minutes they killed eighteen of the *gringos*, wounded many more, and faded away into the mist."

Here Don Enrique stopped, his face pale and his jaws clenched tight, unable to go on, to tell how Ramón de Benivides had suffered a mortal wound at San Pascual and was taken home to die. And how at the moment of his death he swore before the image of Christ on the Cross that revenge would be taken upon the invaders.

"He swore this upon the Cross," Don Enrique managed to say. "And his words have not been forgotten. Revenge upon the *gringos*, now and forever!"

We reached San Miguel at noonday. The rain had ceased but the island was shrouded in mist. No surf was running, so Mr. Dawson and his paraphernalia were put ashore without incident.

Not a word had passed between us during the voyage, nor did we say goodbye. I watched him leave the longboat and climb a trail that wound along the face of a cliff.

He came to the top of the cliff. His hair was blowing in the wind and streamers of mist trailed around him. A vision of Heathcliff came to me, of black-browed Heathcliff standing on the moor looking down upon the place where Cathy Earnshaw dwelt.

4

The Gray
Stone Wall

My father had given Mr. Dawson careful instructions about the search for Cabrillo's grave.

It was to be conducted as secretly as possible. San Miguel was deserted except for a sheepherder or two, but should anyone ask, Mr. Dawson must say that he was an anthropologist digging for fossils. The ship would return for him in exactly five days.

We sailed for Isla del Oro shortly after noon under clearing skies, with a brisk wind astern, and sighted the island at dusk. I had seen little of the mainland except a curtain of blue-gray smog. It was still a mysterious country to me, peopled by strangers, by hordes of *gringos* who had invaded California after the battle of San Pascual. Those upon whom Ramón de Benivides, dying from his wounds, had sworn to be avenged.

Don Enrique read during the voyage home and did not appear until the towers of Castillo Santiago showed in the falling night. Coming to where I stood in the bow of the ship, for a moment he was silent, breathing as if he were in distress. He turned and glanced toward the lighthouse on Point Firmin.

"It flashes green," he said, "an invitation for the unwary to enter. And then it flashes red, a warning to those of wisdom." He touched my arm shyly. "There are two worlds, Lucinda, one is evil and one is not. I protect you as best I can against the world of evil."

He walked away, then came back and was silent again. Then he said, "I have never told you about Isla del Oro. How gold was discovered there. By your grandfather. Before you were born. Have I?"

"No, you haven't."

I was lying. He had told me the story several times, but never the same one twice. I had heard it from my mother and all my tutors and some of the servants when I was very young and liked to be entertained.

Putting all the stories together, they came to this: After the death of Ramón de Benivides, for more than fifty years none of his family set foot upon the island, which was then called Isla Encantada. Not until my grandfather, Don Aurelio, went there on a hunting trip.

On his last day on the island, he was cooking his breakfast on the beach at sunrise. Looking down, he saw a bright pebble lying in the sand. He picked it up, wrapped it in a handkerchief, and took it back to the mainland.

He thought that it might be gold. But he was acquainted with the fate of John Sutter. He knew, as all the world did, how one of Sutter's millworkers, James Marshall, had discovered small pieces of bright metal near the town of Coloma on the American River. And that the two men had tested the metal with nitric acid and proved it to be gold.

In secret, Don Aurelio obtained a vial of this acid and tested the pebble. It was gold, beyond all doubt. Pure gold.

What he found he kept secret, remembering that when news of James Marshall's discovery had reached San Francisco, sailors left their ships, carpenters dropped their hammers, storekeepers boarded up their stores, newspapermen flung down their pens. And everyone headed for the American River.

He also remembered that when the world heard about the discovery, adventurers flocked from everywhere. They staked out every foot of earth in the valley around the town of Coloma. They trampled the vineyards of John Sutter, tore down his mills, destroyed his farms, and made him a pauper.

Don Aurelio remembered this well and kept his secret from everyone, even my grandmother. Only when he lay near death did he call my father to his side and speak about the gold he had found on the beach.

The find remained a secret for years, until a drought killed most of the Santa Gertrudis cattle and the ranch was close to bankruptcy. In desperation, on the chance that where there was a gold pebble there might be a vein of gold nearby, Don Enrique made a voyage to the island. After weeks of searching, he located an outcropping of gold in the face of the blue cliff that rose from Playa Blanca, the cliff upon which Castillo Santiago stands today.

"The pebble your grandfather found on the beach," Don Enrique said, "gave birth to a mine. To three mines. It built Castillo Santiago."

He paused and turned his gaze hard upon me. "And why?" His voice rose to a feverish pitch. "Why, your silence and puzzled eyes ask me. I shall tell you. Listen."

He was silent for a time. When he spoke again his voice was gentle. I could scarcely hear it above the throb of the ship's engines.

"You have not forgotten Ramón de Benivides, your grandfather thrice removed? Good! Then you will remember that he was mortally wounded in battle. That as he lay dying he called down revenge upon those who had slain him. And you know that his oath was not forgotten, but passed on down the years."

His voice rose again. "Castillo Santiago is a token of the

revenge he asked for. But only a token. It stands there on its headland for the invader to see and ponder."

Lights were coming on everywhere in the castle, from the terrace that enclosed it like a battlement to the four square towers soaring off into the night.

Don Enrique had begun the castle when I was a baby and finished it two years before the terrible night my mother fled. He had set it on a headland that rose heavenward in one breathless leap, leaving not so much as a crack or cranny for a gull to nest.

In prehistoric times, the headland had been a spur of the Sierra Nevada range. Where the sea now lay, ferns twice the size of a man flourished, and winged monsters fed upon them. This mountain spur was granite. And of the hard blue stone Castle Santiago was built.

The men who began the great cathedral of Seville said to each other, "Let us build this church in such a way that those who see it will think us mad."

Those who have seen Castillo Santiago, soaring high above the headland, might say the same about my father. He had built a castle of four towers and more than a hundred rooms. Marble colonnades ran its length and led to marble stairways. The galleries that fanned out from these colonnades were paneled with rare woods embossed with gilt mirrors and gold medallions. He had ransacked Europe to furnish his castle with the art of sixteenth-century cabinetmakers. He would have built a moat around the castle, except that it was surrounded by one of the biggest moats in the world, the Pacific Ocean.

Don Enrique clenched his fists and raised them toward the mainland. "The *gringo* will see that it is the mark of our hatred," he said. He left unspoken the last, the most terrible, reason for the hatred that consumed him. But it never went unspoken for long.

There were weeks when he did not go through the ritual, for ritual it was—days when apparently he never thought of it. Then suddenly the urge would come upon him. His face

27

would grow pale. He would seize my arm with a trembling hand, be it day or night, and lead me up the endless stairs, to the topmost floor of the south tower, to the apartment where my mother had once lived.

On this night, no sooner had our carriage left us at the terrace than, in the gentle voice he called upon whenever this madness struck him, he said, using the same words he always used, "Come, my dear, we must see if the wall still stands."

Candles burned in my mother's parlor as they had every night since the night she had disappeared. Their amber light colored everything—the French chairs and the desk she wrote at, the walls of blue brocade. Scarlet flowers of *dama de la noche*, afloat in a crystal bowl, gave off the scent of wild honey.

Holding my arm, Don Enrique led me through the bedroom—undisturbed since the night Francesca de Benivides had left it—into a shadowy alcove lit with one small votive lamp.

On the far side of the alcove, where once a door had opened into a large clothes press, a stone barrier rose from floor to ceiling. It was made of blue granite taken from our mines—in the dim light it looked gray—a barrier of rough stones bound together by black cement.

Don Enrique pointed. "The wall," he said, using the oft-repeated words. "There behind it lie the remains of John Blake, your mother's love." He drew in his breath. "For hours, yes, for days, while I stood here listening, strange sounds, queer mutterings, prolonged and anxious pleas came from behind that wall."

"You could not have imagined them," I said, as he had taught me. "John Blake lies there. He did not escape?"

"No," Don Enrique cried.

"You could not have imagined the moans and pleadings?"

"Never! Never!"

John Wesley Blake had come to the island years before.

In a winter's gale his white sailing sloop had been driven ashore two miles south of the castle. He was found in the cabin of his grounded boat, nearly dead, rescued by Captain Vega and taken to the mine hopsital where he was slowly nursed back to health.

I never saw or heard of Mr. Blake during those weeks. I only met him later because of his unusual profession. He was an artist, a painter of portraits, and in the hospital he found the strength to do a portrait of one of my mother's maids.

Usually the dozens of young and old beachcombers, gold prospectors, and health seekers who got themselves on the island were promptly removed by Captain Vega. But my mother was enthralled by the portrait. She also liked Mr. Blake, his odd ways and shaggy appearance. My father disliked him, not only because he was a *gringo* but also because he tried his best to paint like Goya, the peerless Spaniard.

"If there had been no Francisco José de Goya y Lucientes," my father would say, "then there would be no John Wesley Blake."

"I would rather own a copy of a painting by a first-rate artist," my mother would reply, "than an original by a fourth-rate artist."

There were more arguments of this kind, but my mother always won. This is how John Blake was engaged to do my portrait and why he moved into the castle, bringing with him his salvaged brushes and paint and canvas.

With the snobbery of a spoiled child who always mistook shadow for substance, I was repelled by his shaggy appearance and paid him scant attention. But later he sat on the bench beside me while I performed a piece my mother requested, and when he complimented me upon my playing, I warmed to him a little.

Mr. Blake didn't begin on me at once. He spent a day studying Murillo's portrait of Teresa de Benivides and two days following me around.

"I would like to form some idea of Miss Lucinda's personality," he said to my mother. "She's very changeable—gloomy one moment, happy the next."

"Lucinda's really a happy child," my mother said. "I want a happy picture." She hesitated for a moment. "I have seen you studying the Murillo."

"Yes, I find that your daughter has the same smile as the girl in the picture. It's an engaging smile. Quite beautiful."

"Not beautiful," my mother said. "*Unique* is the better word." She put a finger on her chin, thinking. "Can you change it somehow?"

"A three-quarters view," he said, "her body turned, will change the smile."

It took him the better part of a month to paint my portrait. There were two one-hour sittings every day, which annoyed Don Enrique. He hated John Blake and was jealous, I think, that my mother came to watch him paint.

She said she came to keep me company, but she didn't come for that reason. She came because she had fallen in love with John Wesley Blake.

She gave a wonderful fiesta for the islanders when my portrait was finished. Lanterns lit the terrace. Searchlights from the *Infanta* swept the sky. Food came from the burning coals in a savory stream. A mariachi band, brought from somewhere in Mexico, that didn't sound the way mariachis usually do—like a load of empty tin cans rattling down a chute—played and the guests danced.

I wore my pink silk dresss, which had white lace from the Calle Serpientes around the neck, and black slippers with pure gold buckles. I wanted to wear a blue knit dress with a yellow underskirt that my mother had ordered for me from Salazar in Madrid. But Don Enrique thought it was *demasiada arrojada,* too bold for a girl of eight.

Toward midnight the marimbas sounded a flourish from "El Rancho Grande." Mother unveiled my portrait, and everyone applauded. Then the band played a waltz and I danced for a few minutes with John Wesley Blake. His face was flushed and he had a far-away look. I thought it was because everyone except my father was pleased with his work. I was wrong, very wrong and innocent.

After two hours or more, probably near two-thirty in the morning, when the fiesta was at its merriest, I noticed that my mother had disappeared. From Mercedes I learned that she had been taken ill soon after the portrait was unveiled, and had gone upstairs. Worried, because she wasn't strong, I went to find out what I could do to please her.

As I reached her door I heard a loud voice, my father's, angrily shouting the name *John Blake*. Between shouts there was the sound of people moving around. Of hammers striking stone. Another shout, this one directed at Francesca de Cabrillo y Benivides, each word dragged out contemptuously.

Farther along the hall a clock slowly struck the hour of three. I stood and listened, too frightened to move. Suddenly the door was flung open and my mother fled past me, down the corrodor, and was gone. After a dreadful moment Don Enrique stood in the doorway.

"Come," he said. "Come, I wish to show you what is happening to the lover of Francesca de Cabrillo y Benivides."

"Come!" he repeated as I pulled back, about to flee, and took me by the arm.

Don Enrique guided me through the sitting room to the bed, his fingers biting into my arm. Here he stopped and pointed to the massive clothes press at the far end of the alcove.

The two ebony doors with their gold bands and gold knobs were closed. In front of them were a huge pile of stones and barrows filled with what looked to be cement. Two miners were building a wall. Already it stood more than waist high, the gray stone shining silvery in the light of their smoking lamps.

"*Señor* Blake," my father said, "stands behind the doors. Or sits. Or lies. But there, nonetheless."

On the bed beside us lay the portrait John Wesley Blake had painted, its gold frame broken, the canvas slashed with a knife.

"He is there," my father said. "There forever."

I wanted to scream, but didn't. I gasped for breath and ran. I ran out of the room, down the endless flight of stairs into the night. A carriage was leaving the driveway, moving away toward the harbor. In the light from the carriage lamp I caught a fleeting glimpse of my mother's face. I called to her. In answer, she raised her hand in farewell.

The ritual was half over. Now my father led me downstairs, through a windowless passageway that ran along one side of the south wing and ended at the massive doors of the chapel. A servant was always there, day and night. The door was opened. We went to the altar, knelt before it, and prayed our separate and secret prayers.

The ritual was over.

On the north wall near the ceiling was a latticed opening that looked down into the chapel. Behind this opening Don Enrique had his sleeping quarters—a bare wooden floor and a narrow bed with a figure of Christ above it. He could lie in bed and look down through a peephole in the lattice at the carved wooden benches, those he had brought from a nunnery in Spain. Upon a statue of the Virgin that was said to have miraculous powers. Upon those who came and went.

We parted without a word. My father disappeared. As I left the chapel I saw his face pressed against the latticed window. His eyes were following me.

The ritual, accustomed though I was to the violent act, had never affected me more than on this night. The excitement of the voyage to San Miguel, the brief glimpses of a world I didn't know and perhaps never would know, the beginning of the search for Cabrillo's grave—all had conspired to upset me. I was expected for dinner, as usual, but I sent word by my maid that I was ill. She came back grim-faced.

Mercedes Ochoa was more than a maid. She was a friend, one of the few I had among the servants. She had come to the island from Avila in Spain, where she served as the custodian of a destroyed nunnery, from which Don Enrique had taken the chapel benches and the dining-room table, which seated more than sixty guests. Impressed with her skill at bargaining, he had brought her to Isla del Oro.

"Don Enrique is not pleased," Mercedes told me. "He is disappointed in his daughter. He suggests that she take some of the medicine Dr. Wolfe had prescribed for her. The three men from the mine are coming to play their guitars and he wishes her to play the harpsichord. He is waiting. Should I select a dress for you, the blue one?"

"I am not going to dinner," I said.

Mercedes was clutching a sconce filled with candles, otherwise she would have wrung her hands. She had a long, narrow face and deep hollows in her cheeks. The candlelight made the hollows deeper.

"What do you wish to say?" she asked.

"That I am ill and will remain so."

Mercedes was gone only a short time. She returned to say that Don Enrique had fallen silent when he received the news, but that he was angry—very, very angry.

"I am sorry that he's very, very angry," I said, but I didn't feel sorry.

"You are ill from today," Mercedes said. "I have noticed more and more these last months that you become ill after he takes you there and talks about the wall."

She put the candles down and clasped her hands together. She was scarcely speaking above a whisper.

"I know this is not the time to say something that has been on my mind. But the servants—I don't know which one, I think it's Elena, the new girl, who started it—they're saying that there are two people behind the wall. A man and a woman."

"Who could the woman possibly be?"

Mercedes wrung her hands.

"Who?" I demanded.

"Forgive me," she said. "They say it is your mother."

33

"It can't be! The night that it all happened I was there. I saw my mother leave the room. Run down the stairs. I saw her with my own eyes. She can't be behind the wall."

"Forgive me," Mercedes said. "I thought you should know about the rumors. What the servants are saying."

"Tell Elena, the new one, and all the rest to stop the talk about my mother."

"I will tell them, Elena first," Mercedes said.

"Tell them now," I said. "Tonight before they go to bed."

I lay down to sleep but did not close my eyes. The tide was running on the rocks below, softly in and out like a wounded animal breathing. Surely the servants were wrong. They loved to gossip. I had seen my mother flee out of the door and down the corridor into the night. Yet she could have returned to the castle. Don Enrique or someone might have forced her to return. It was possible that she lay behind the gray wall. In horror I got to my feet and ran to the window. The sky was starless, streaked with gray clouds. A gray mist covered the cliff and the beach.

I was roused from my stupor by the sound of guitars. The three men were playing music they had written for the words of a Lorca poem—*"Mariposa de luz, mariposa de luz"*—butterfly of light.

Someone was speaking to me in the poem. The voice was familiar. It was someone I had known long ago.

I unbarred the door, crossed the corridor, and stood for a while, staring into the shadowed well that wound down and down, floor after floor, straining to hear the words.

I went down the stairs like someone walking in her sleep, drawn by the sound of the tender voice, and stood in the doorway, a sleepwalker—with hair falling around my face. There were people in the room, but I didn't see them. I didn't see Don Enrique until he grasped my shoulder.

"You are disturbed," he whispered. "Leave!"

I did not move. The voice was saying my name. It called to me from another day.

34

Words rose unbidden to my lips. "Mother!" I said.

Don Enrique tightened his grip on my shoulder.

"Your mother is gone," he said in a hoarse whisper. "Let her be. Do not speak her name in my hearing ever again!" He gave me a shove. "Go!"

I steadied myself. I did not move until the song ended. Then I turned away and left the room. As I reached the top of the staris I heard footsteps behind me.

Father Martínez said in his gravelly voice, "Let's take a moment and look at a different world. This one is out of kilter."

Holding his candle aloft, he led me down the long, dark corridor that connected the two towers and into his quarters, half of which was a sorry jumble of clothes and books—he forbade the maids to touch his things—and the other half a domelike room that housed a telescope.

"I heard you call your mother," he said. "It is best to heed Don Enrique's warning. She is gone and you cannot bring her back."

"But *is* she gone?"

"What are you saying?"

"That she's behind the wall."

"A rumor. There were many at the time. Some persist."

"You could have the wall torn down," I said. "And end the rumors."

"Not without Don Enrique's permission. I have asked him before. He says that it will not come down until doomsday. Not an hour before the trumpet blows."

He got to his knees and I knelt beside him. He said a rambling prayer. I didn't pray, nor did I listen. Afterward he went to one of his cabinets and took out an iron crank, which he put in a slot and turned.

Magically, as he cranked the vaulted roof opened like a clamshell, revealing the sky. I had watched it open many times before, always with wonder. This night I watched with dull eyes.

"I am getting a little old for this business," Father Martínez said. "Someday we will have electricity, I hope."

The telescope, high in the center of the dome, was reached by a ladder that wound upward like a corkscrew to a small platform. He started up the ladder and motioned for me to follow.

Agile as a spider, he had already reached the platform and was adjusting the eyepiece when I got there.

"We'll have a glance at Hercules 13M," he said. "It's not spectacular."

I looked into the eyepiece. "It's like a thumbprint."

"Like God's thumbprint," Father Martínez said. "Yet it is a fiery collection of suns. One hundred thousand suns. All of them larger than our sun."

He waited for me to say something, but I couldn't think of anything more than that it looked like a thumbprint. So he turned the telescope to bring in red Antares and ice-blue Sirius and the spinning galaxies deep in the night, trying to coax from my mind the thoughts of the gray stone wall and all that it concealed.

He gave up at last and I went back to my tower and to bed. I dreamed that a pink and black bushmaster came to my window up from the rocks. It looked in at me, swishing its tail like the sound of distant castanets, its forked black tongue tasting the air and, using words I barely understood, begged to be let in.

5

Jennifer's Mistake

In five days—it might have been longer because this was a disturbing time—my father sailed back to San Miguel.

The ship was barely on its way when Jennifer Delaney appeared. She had never been here before. As I have said, we were forbidden to talk more than was necessary, and she was not to visit the tower for any reason. This rule of conduct, one of many laid down by my father, was meant to protect me from contamination. (It puzzled me why he brought only *gringas* to the island, yet forbade me to associate with them.)

Jennifer knocked at the door. She did not wait for an answer but burst into the middle of the room. She glanced around at my nunlike cell—at the straight-back chair that Saint Teresa once had used, at a painting of the saint, at the narrow bed with its small, hard pillows.

Beyond this room was a smaller one, where I kept my books. It had an oblong window, more like a porthole in a ship. She looked out across the channel.

"What's that?" she asked. "An island?"

"The mainland," I said, "what you can see of it."

Jennifer glanced at the bookshelves. "You must read a lot, like your father." She examined the titles. "Charles Dickens' *David Copperfield* . . . *La Circe* by Lope de Vega . . . *Vanity Fair* by William Makepeace Thackeray . . . Whew, what a name!" She turned away. Don't you have something romantic? A mystery? Something new?"

I told her that Don Enrique forbade me to read anything new, any book written in this century, by any author from any country. Or magazines. Or newspapers.

"Like a shipless sailor, the world wobbles drunkenly to its doom," he said. "Thieves roam the streets where even nuns aren't safe. Idiot chatter befouls the air. The mindless sit and watch shadows come and go. Greed is God and Sex is Queen. Satan himself cruises the highways with a bottle in his hand."

Don Enrique said and feverently believed that we must turn back the clock of centuries. Before it is too late, we must return to long ago, to the Age of Faith.

I was tempted to repeat this to Jennifer, but since what my father believed was none of her business I merely said, "You might like Sir Walter Scott's *Ivanhoe*, or *Kenilworth*, perhaps."

"I'm not much of a reader," Jennifer said. "I like TV, but there's none in the castle. Is there any on the island?"

"No."

"Radio?"

"Only on the *Infanta*. There was one in the village last year. One of the miners had it. But he never turned it off and Don Enrique had it destroyed."

"Your father watches everything on the island," Jennifer said.

"It is his island," I said.

"He watches you, too."

"I am his daughter," I said bluntly.

Not at all rebuffed, Jennifer said, "It must be a bore. This morning I saw you out walking in the garden and trailing along behind you, practically stepping on your heels, was one of Captain Vega's *pistoleros*. And behind him were two more *pistoleros*. I suppose there were a dozen I didn't see, lurking in the rosebushes. I saw you stoop to pick a flower and you caught your dress on a thorn or something, and a maid ran out from somewhere and got you loose.''

''That's not so unusual,'' I said, piqued by her tone. ''When Lucrezia d'Este walked in her garden she had a much larger entourage. When she left Rome once to go on a journey, she was accompanied by twenty ladies-in-waiting, a secretary, a majordomo, three chaplains, servants, cooks, keepers of the wardrobe, ten grooms, tailors, a reader of books, fifty muleteers, one cardinal, three bishops, two hundred soldiers, four Spanish clowns, and twenty trumpeteers with jeweled trumpets.''

Jennifer was not listening. She picked up a pair of binoculars from the window ledge and fixed them upon the *Infanta*, which had passed the Narrows and was turning north toward San Miguel island.

She watched the ship until it was out of sight. ''Do you go out on dates?'' she said. ''I guess not, come to think of it. There's no one on Isla del Oro to date.''

I let her stare at me for a while. Then I said in a matter-of-fact tone, ''I don't go out on dates because I'm engaged.''

''Engaged? Really? Who is it? Not that Captain Vega with his little pointed beard and lizard eyes?''

''The Captain is married,'' I said and went into the bedroom and brought back an album, which I laid on the windowsill where the light was best.

There were dozens of pictures of my *novio*—a fat-faced baby in a crib decorated with ribbons and lace, a boy on his knees before an altar, a young man on a spirited Arabian horse. Also a picture of him seated on an iron bench beside his parents. It was loose in the album. (I had never gotten around to pasting it down.) And one of him in court attire that hung on the wall.

39

"His name is Porfirio," I said. "Porfirio Puerto-blanca. He is the son of the Duke and Duchess of Alicante y Vallecitos."

"Hmmm," Jennifer muttered. "When are you getting married?"

"Porfirio hasn't graduated yet," I said. "He has three more years at the university. So we'll have to wait."

"Does he like Isla del Oro?"

"He's never been here."

"When did you see him?"

"I never have seen him."

"Except in these pictures?"

"Yes. But my father's talked to his parents. Everything is arranged."

I closed the album and put it away, feeling remiss for not pasting down the picture of Porfirio and his parents. It wasn't a very good picture, as a matter of fact. It made him look not so dashing as he did from a distance riding on the horse. Up close his face looked too fat and his sideburns too long.

Jennifer was silent. I took that to mean she was not impressed with Porfirio.

"I don't think much of this custom of being engaged to someone you don't know and haven't even seen," she said. "And I've heard that you Spanish girls are chaperoned from the cradle until the day you're married. That's another custom I don't like. But it does save a lot of unwed girls from having children."

"My father has told me that more than half a million teenagers had illegitimate children last year. He says that when they're not busy having children, they smoke marijuana, watch TV, drive around town in their parents' car, argue with them a lot, listen to records, and sulk."

"I see you have a player," Jennifer said. She went over and flipped through the cabinet. "Mozart . . . Vivaldi . . . Chopin . . . Whew! Nothing else? I brought some along—

Barry Manilow and Donna Summer and the Eagles. We'll play them sometime. Tonight, maybe."

It would not be tonight or any night, but I didn't tell her so. She would find out soon enough that jazz and rock were forbidden. And a lot of other things, too, as the others had learned. The others? For a long time I had wondered how and where Don Enrique found the young women who came to Isla del Oro.

Jennifer was so sure of herself, that I was emboldened to say, "How did you hear about the island?"

"Through a newspaper. The *New York Daily News*. I lived in New Jersey but I read this ad. I wrote six letters to your father and got six back before I found out about all his requirements."

I had a general idea of what the requirements were just from observing the women who had come to the island, but I asked her about them anyway.

"He wanted a non-Catholic, young—between the ages of twenty and twenty-five . . ."

Jennifer looked seventeen or eighteen, nineteen at the most, so she must have lied about her age.

"Your relatives and friends shouldn't be the nosy type, wanting to visit the island and so forth. You should have a good education. High shcool, anyway. And a skill."

"What is yours?" I said. "I know that you write a beautiful hand."

"That's it, a beautiful hand," Jennifer said. "But also you must be attractive, slender blondes preferred. And a color photograph to prove it. I sent three. One in a pink evening dress. One in a street dress and one in a white bikini—I had a good tan at the time that I got down in Coney Island and the contrast between the white suit and my mahogany skin was very, very . . ."

"Striking," I said when she couldn't think of a word.

All of the women—eighteen by count—who had arrived on the island since my mother had fled were very pretty. And yet not one of them, from what I had seen and more importantly from what the servants had seen and reported, had ever become my father's mistress.

"There were a lot more things," Jennifer went on. "Kooky things like 'how many baths do you take each day?' I said two, figuring he was a nut on baths, although sometimes I forget to take even one."

She stood at the window gazing out toward the mainland. Her blonde hair looked golden in the morning sun. I wondered how long it would be until the day the *Infanta* carried her back to the mainland. No longer than two months, I guessed, for Jennifer was much like Melanie Morse, who didn't like to eat with the servants and said so. Nor did she look pleased when my father said that she could eat at our table on Sundays. And made a courtly bow and kissed her hand. They were both prideful women.

Jennifer came back late that afternoon with three of her records. "That's another kooky thing," she said. "In the last letter I got from your father he told me that there was no electricity on the island. So I had to trade my player in on a battery model. Crazy."

She put her records on the turntable. I reminded her about the rules of Castillo Santiago, none of which—the rules or my reminding her about them—she liked.

In a huff she went to the window and was gazing longingly out at the hazy line of the mainland coast when the *Infanta* sailed through the Narrows and docked at the wharf. I watched through the binoculars as my father and Mr. Dawson came down the gangplank.

Mr. Dawson hadn't changed. He was still tall and long-haired and wildly romantic, exactly as Heathcliff must have seemed to Cathy Earnshaw when she glanced out the window and saw him coming through the meadow.

"What do you see?" Jennifer asked, taking the glasses.

"Don Enrique," I said. "And Mr. Heathcliff."

"Heathcliff?" she said. "It's Dawson. Who is Heathcliff?"

Embarrassed, I didn't try to explain who he was.

"They've got a yellow box. Four men carrying it," Jennifer said. "It looks like a coffin."

"It is a coffin."

"Who's dead?"

"Admiral Juan Rodriguez Cabrillo."

Four men put the yellow coffin in a wagon and they started off toward the village. Our village is clustered around the harbor and the miners' huts line both sides of the road. As the wagon appeared, the miners came out and watched it pass. They stood in the twilight with their heads uncovered until it went through the iron gates that carried the Benivides crest and the red and yellow flag of Spain.

"Who's Cabrillo?" Jennifer asked.

"My ancestor. He died four hundred and forty years ago and discovered this island. He was buried on San Miguel, an island to the north of us."

Jennifer stared at me. "Cabrillo was dug up? He's in that yellow box? Why?"

"It's my father's wish that he lie here among his friends."

"I understand," Jennifer said, but it was clear that she didn't. "He'll be buried on Isla del Oro?"

"Here in the castle." The room was dark by now and I got up and lit a candle. It could have been the yellow light that made her face look pale. "In our crypt," I said.

"When?"

"I don't know. Soon, most likely."

"Will there be a funeral?"

"A funeral and a fiesta. Don Enrique always celebrates death. It's more important to him than birth."

Jennifer left the room, but in a few moments she was back, carrying a bundle of phonograph records. "It's gloomy in here. Like a tomb," she said and put her records on the turntable. "Let's hear a cheer for our side."

The record turned slowly, giving off strange sounds made by a guitar and drums and some kind of a horn. Jennifer began to dance, tossing her arms and bending her knees in awkward positions, rolling her eyes, breathing through her mouth, licking her lips. Sweat began to glisten on her forehead.

She knew the rules of Castillo Santiago, because I had told her. I was surprised that she would flout them, even though my father was out of earshot down in the driveway, talking to the driver of the wagon that held the yellow box. I was not Jennifer's chaperone, or her mother.

The record wound to a close with drum beats and a wailing voice. There was a knock at the door. Before I could move, Don Enrique slipped in and carefully closed the door behind him.

For a moment he stood listening to the voice singing, "Physical, physical, let's get physical." After the words were repeated four or five times, as if the needle were stuck, he strode over, lifted the record from the turntable, walked to the window and was about to toss it, when he changed his mind, put it back on the turntable, gathered up the machine, my machine, and tossed everything through the window. Then, without a word, he left, slamming the door behind him.

6

Visions

Two days later, invitations, written by Jennifer in her elegant script, were delivered to the superintendents of the mines, the engineers in charge of smelting, the captain and lieutenant of the *pistoleros*, the village mayordomo. To these, their families, and a few others of lesser standing, the gold-embossed cards were delivered by hand. No replies were expected. Each invitation was a command.

The guests came in a sober mood, not knowing whether they were to attend one of the gala fiestas that Don Enrique gave when the spirit seized him, or to receive bad news, which he often reserved for these occasions. He believed that it was better if the guests arrived in a sober mood, not knowing what to expect. Bad news was then easier to accept and pleasure had a keener edge.

At the close of the dinner, which was sumptuous, Don Enrique got to his feet. For a time he stood in silence, his eyes burning with an unnatural light. The table was quiet. The servants stood rigid in their places.

"We are here," Don Enrique said, "to honor Juan Rodri-

45

guez Cabrillo, servant of God, discoverer of this island and all the islands hereabouts.''

A reverent sigh that you could not hear but could feel passed through the room. At this moment a tremor shook Don Enrique. I tried to imagine Cabrillo alive. The name means "little goat." So Juan must have resembled a goat—a small figure with a tuft of hair growing low on his forehead, a beard, and a goat's wise, yellow eyes.

"Long had Admiral Cabrillo lain on a windswept hill," my father went on, "in a desolate place, his grave unknown, his only companion the birds of the air. Now that time has ended. Tonight Juan Rodriguez Cabrillo, Admiral of the Ocean Seas, rests in peace on this island, home at last among friends and *compadres*."

He raised his glass and invited everyone to join him. He summoned the singers. A small band of servants in white robes appeared and sang the Te Deum as they circled the table. Candles were given to all of us and we joined the procession, Don Enrique leading the way, down the staircase that wound with many turnings deep into the earth, to the crypt beneath the castle.

A hundred candles burned on the altar, a thousand around the marble walls, which were the color of a damask rose. The crypt was ablaze with candlelight.

In its center, on a chalcedony bed, lay the remains of Juan Rodriguez Cabrillo, covered with flowers. His helmet and steel breastplate lay at his feet, beside his damascened sword. His name was carved at the foot of the catafalque and the day of his birth and death.

After Father Martínez had read the requiem mass, and had said in his deepest voice, *"Dominus vobiscum,"* the throng scrambled up the stairs to drink more wine and eat dessert. Don Enrique asked me to enliven the party with some eighteenth-century tunes on the harpsichord. Then he disappeared into the library, taking with him Christopher Dawson.

Mr. Dawson had not been invited to dinner and was not

present at the burial, so I was surprised to see him. I was more surprised later when he came out of the library while I was still playing and sauntered across the room.

I wouldn't have known that he was suddenly behind me, except that I saw his reflection in the windowpane—a dark, mysterious figure towering above me in the dim light.

I was playing a piece from a seventeenth-century masque, a tripping *zarzuela* that was quite simple—at least compared with the Mozart I had just finished. My fingers were raised to make a final, sweeping arpeggio, when the keyboard wavered and seemed to float away. My fingers faltered in midair. Against my will, they then swooped down, not in a series of delicate notes, but in an ugly, crashing chord.

I heard a sympathetic word spoken in a whisper. I felt a hand on my naked shoulder. It was there for only a moment. My face began to burn. I glanced up. He stood there above me, gazing at the portrait of Teresa de Cabrillo y Benivides.

"You look like this girl," he said. "It's the eyes. The eyes and the smile."

"The smile," I said.

"Yes, the smile more than anything. She must be related."

"She is. From long ago. Centuries ago."

"Strange how the genes transport beauty from one generation to another," he said, "preserving it through hundreds of years.'

His words were spoken in a deep tone and slowly. My throat had closed and I couldn't answer.

Then a hoarse, demanding voice spoke at my elbow. "You have played well, especially the *zarzuela*," my father said. "Everyone has enjoyed your music. It is now time for bed."

He took my arm firmly, brushed past Mr. Dawson, and led me to the landing. There he patted my hand and bade me goodnight.

I went up the stairs but did not go to bed. I snuffed out the candles and stood in the dark looking out at the sea and the glittering lights.

The half moon that showed in the east had moved high overhead when I heard a soft knock, twice repeated. Jennifer had not been at the dinner or the burial and I hadn't seen her since Don Enrique tossed my record player out the window, so I went to the door expecting that she had come to complain about how shabbily she was being treated.

The lamps in the passageway blinded me for a moment. I then made out the tall figure of a man I took to be my father. It was Mr. Dawson. He came in without an invitation and closed the door quietly behind him. I ran to light a candle.

"You're frightened," he said.

"You did frighten me," I managed to say.

I was still frightened. I couldn't imagine why he had come here. Scenes from books I had read flashed past my eyes—of Robert Lovelace, rake and seducer, pursuing Clarissa Harlowe to her ruin; of the evil Tarquinius, inflamed with Lucrece's beauty, stealing by night into her unguarded chamber.

"It was not my intention," Mr. Dawson said, "to frighten you."

My fears lessened somewhat by these words. I nevertheless went to the door and stood ready to open it.

Taken aback, Mr. Dawson stood in the middle of the room, his hands at his sides, and said nothing.

Emboldened by his silence, I said angrily, "If one of the servants has seen you enter this room, it will turn out badly for you. And for me. What will I say if someone appears at the door? Do you have any ideas?"

Mr. Dawson had none. He remained silent. For an instant I thought that he was about to leave.

"I came here to say goodbye," he said.

In my anger, not waiting to learn what he meant by "goodbye," I said, "You could have done that downstairs."

"I hadn't a chance," Mr. Dawson said. "You remember

how your father dragged you off as soon as he saw us talking together."

He didn't move, but stood surveying me. They were blasting in one of the mines and the sound echoed in the room. He waited until it was quiet again.

"Your father has a new idea," he said. "He wants me to find Gaspar de Portolá's grave. Portolá is the conquistador who came up from Mexico in 1776 or thereabouts and explored the country as far north as San Francisco."

"I've heard of him," I said. I could have said that Don Enrique owned a dozen books about Portolá and that I had read every one of them.

"The grave is in Mexico," Mr. Dawson went on. "In Sinaloa. Your father wants me to go there and bring back Portolá's bones. He plans to bury them in the crypt beside Juan Cabrillo.

"The *Infanta* will take me to San Diego," he said. "I'll fly from there."

Mr. Dawson bowed as he had seen my father bow—a slight dip of the chin—and held out his hand.

It was the first time in my life that I had felt a man's hand in mine. Except for my father's, which was hard and cold as though he were wearing an iron glove.

He walked toward the door. Trying to think of something appropriate to say, I opened it and stepped aside to let him pass. He closed the door and stood with his back against it.

"I like you," he said. "And I fear for you. The island is a prison and you are a prisoner. You can't be happy. Are you?"

"Yes," I said, lying. "Very happy, Mr. Dawson."

"My name is Christopher," he said, correcting me, then, "You are waited upon day and night and guarded while you sleep."

The candlelight threw his shadow against the door, tall and unmoving, and again frightening.

"You're treated like a child, like a little princess, and you seem to enjoy it very much. But you are being smothered.

49

They are killing you." He paused. "I start tomorrow on your father's demented mission. The *Infanta* leaves early. You should leave the island . . . you must."

Again the sound of blasting echoed in the room. Then it was very quiet. I heard steps moving away down the hall. Someone had been listening at the door. It could have been Alicia. More likely it was Villaverde, Don Enrique's favorite servant.

Christopher had heard the footsteps, too. He took my hands in his and kissed my face. Then he opened the door and was gone. I followed him to the stairwell and watched him go down the stairs, hearing his steps like my own heartbeats, until he disappeared.

Moving in a dream, I closed the door. I put out the candle and lay down to sleep. I was no longer in Castillo Santiago. I was thousands of miles away, standing in a crowded railroad station as Prince Vronsky and Anna Karenina met again.

I saw the snow flying from the carriage roofs as the engine whistled plaintively. I felt Anna's joy at seeing Vronsky, a joy I hadn't felt when I read Tolstoi's story. I heard her ask him why he had followed her from St. Petersburg, why he was on the same train she was on.

I heard him answer, while the storm raged, looking straight into her eyes, "What am I coming for? You know that I have come to be where you are."

Like Anna on the train that was taking her away after she and Vronsky had parted, I did not sleep all night. Like hers, the visions that filled my thoughts were blissful and glowing. And when I finally dozed toward morning, I dreamed that I was at Christopher's side and he was taking me away from Isla del Oro.

7

Escape

The day dawned bright. Beyond the channel on the mainland coast the beaches and cliffs and blue mountains shone clear. The *Infanta* lay at the wharf, smoke rising from her stacks, her flags standing out in the wind. My mind was made up.

I turned Porfirio's fat face to the wall, dressed quickly, and went down the servants' stairs to the chapel. The caretaker had just opened the doors, and Father Martínez was lighting candles. I called good morning to him, but didn't stay to talk.

I made a hurried curtsy before the altar. The Virgin of the Sea, the sweet-faced Mother of Christ, radiant in her golden crown and strings of gleaming pearls, in her lacy gown of gold and ribbons, looked down upon me.

I prayed but the words came painfully.

"Beautiful Virgin of Isla del Oro," I prayed, "in your infinite wisdom comfort my mother, wherever she is, and may it be far from this island in a happier place. Will you please protect my father from evil chance and the consequences of wrongful pride. And will you please, dear Virgin, watch over me as I begin this journey . . ."

When I rose Father Martínez was standing beside me. "Your knees must be stiff," he said. "You have been there for a long time." He searched my face. "You look pale, as if you had not slept. Does something trouble you?"

"Nada."

"Is there something you wish to confess?"

"No, Father."

"You're certain?"

"Yes."

"We were supposed to have a lesson last night," he said. "It will be given tonight. And, *señorita,* kindly bring your notebook." He pointed his finger. "Oh, I know you pride yourself on being able to read a whole page and say it back from memory, but bring your notebook anyway."

I had a twinge of regret that tonight I would not sit in his musty tower that smelled of snuff and perique, listening to him talk about the stars. Or look through the big telescope, trading my earthly vision for its great, encompassing eye. Not tonight and perhaps not ever again.

Our servants were gathering at the altar in their black skirts and stiff, white blouses, whispering their first prayers of the day. I said goodbye to Father Martínez. As I passed under the latticed window that looked down from my father's bedroom at the altar and the Virgin of the Sea, the peephole that he had copied from King Philip's bedroom in the Escorial, I glanced up.

By now the chapel was filled with smoke from the rows of votive candles. It was difficult to see, but I made out the muzzle and lolling tongue of a staghound. The dog's head faded out, leaving a mist upon the glass. Then suddenly my father's gaunt face appeared, his eyes fixed upon me.

He had been watching, I was certain, during the time I had knelt at the altar. He knew that I never came to the chapel at this early hour. He knew that I would never kneel on the hard marble floor for such a long time unless something was amiss.

The face at the window drew back and the gray staghound was watching me again. I hurried on, expecting that when I reached the chapel door my father would be outside waiting for me. He was not there.

Taking the back stairs, I raced to the fourth floor and after a frantic search found Mercedes Ochoa.

"I need a servant's uniform," I told her. "Everything —underclothes, a dress, shoes, and stockings."

Mercedes must have been surprised, but she didn't show it.

"And sunglasses," I said. I had a dozen pair, but all of them were in odd shapes and colors—nothing that one of our servants would be allowed to wear. "And please hurry."

She didn't ask why I wanted the clothes. Without a word, she found the sizes she thought would suit me. I hastily undressed and put them on. Everything fit except the shoes, which were too small and pinched my feet.

"Did you come to the door last night?" I asked her. "I heard sounds in the hallway. Around midnight."

"No, not then," Mercedes said. "Not after dinner."

She was honest, I trusted her, so it was someone else who had stopped at my door to listen.

"If anyone asks, say you don't know where I am. You haven't seen me since early morning."

"Even your father?"

"Even him."

Carrying nothing except a string bag that belonged to Mercedes, I set off on foot for the harbor. Dressed in a long blue dress and ground-gripper shoes, my hair done up in a blue scarf, dark glasses hiding my eyes, I looked like any of the other servants walking down to the village. I knew my disguise was complete when I was whistled at by miners on their way to work, something they would not have dared to do had they recognized me.

In the village the little stores were just beginning to open.

I waved to all the storekeepers but did not speak. The ship lay at her mooring, gray smoke drifting up from her stacks. The gangplank was down and two of her crew were walking the deck. I looked up and down the wharf. Christopher was nowhere in sight.

An armored wagon drove up while I stood trying to make up my mind whether to board the ship. It was the day gold was being shipped to the mainland. *Pistoleros* with guns in their belts set about unloading the heavy bars. Captain Vega, dressed in a three-cornered hat and a tight black uniform—he wore a leather corset—watched, his boots and pearl-handled pistols agleam in the sun. Now and then he cast a glance in my direction.

I waited in the shadow of the warehouse. Captain Vega and his six *pistoleros* filed aboard the ship. Captain Wolfe began to pace the bridge, pausing to look up at the castle. As the ship's bell struck four times, for the hour of ten, a carriage came rumbling out of the castle grounds and down the steep grade.

I couldn't tell who was in the carriage. I stepped behind a stack of wooden boxes where I could see but not be readily seen. I felt certain that Don Enrique had followed me.

But it was Christopher who opened the door, who jumped down and ran up the gangplank, toting a bag on his shoulders. As he reached the deck he glanced back at the wharf— the only sign that he thought I might be waiting—then disappeared.

There was a long blast from the *Infanta's* horn. Sailors stood by, ready to cast off the lines. Forgetting that I was a servant, I walked sedately toward the ship. A second blast from the air horn reminded me that I was not Lucinda de Cabrillo y Benivides, for whom the ship would wait an hour if necessary.

I hurried, but as I put my foot on the gangway an invisible hand held me back. For a moment a sharp pain gripped my arm. Again, after many years, I felt the steel bracelet on my wrist, the chain that had bound me to my nurse. Now it was not a nurse who held me, but my father. I saw his gaunt face at the window, his dark eyes looking down at me as I left the chapel. I could not move.

A third blast sounded from the *Infanta's* horn. From high on the bridge, Captain Wolfe glanced below at the servant who dared to delay the ship. He lifted a megaphone and sent a round, Spanish curse in my direction.

Still I didn't move. I was rooted, one foot on the wharf and one on the gangway. Above me on the deck loomed the tall figure of Christopher Dawson. He was leaning on the ship's rail, looking down at me.

"What's wrong, lady?" he called out, not recognizing me in servant's clothes. "Can I be of help?"

I did not answer him. I couldn't, but the chain that held me loosened. Suddenly it fell from my wrist. I was free, free. I ran up the gangway. When I reached the deck Christopher was nowhere in sight.

Women dressed in their Sunday best stood at the far rail, their backs turned toward me. I recognized two of them as our servants. (Don Enrique permitted each of the servants to spend one day a year on the mainland.) To avoid them I moved away toward the stern of the ship.

With another blast from the horn, the lines came in, and we slowly headed for the Narrows. Looking back, I could see the castle high on the cliff, its turrets and four towers —my own tower with its one window facing the east—the copper roofs smoldering red in the morning sun.

There was no sign of life on the terraces, nor on the tree-bordered road that ran steeply down into the village. Yet I did not feel safe until the ship swung out into the open sea.

8

Farewell to Freedom

I found a place at the stern of the ship sheltered from the wind and the eyes of Captain Wolfe. He hadn't recognized me as I stood on the gangway, but if we met now and he did recognize me, he would turn the ship around and take me back to Isla del Oro.

Castillo Santiago faded away in the mist. The island grew smaller. I didn't expect that Christopher would look for me. Like Captain Wolfe, he hadn't seen through my makeshift disguise as I stood on the gangway and desperately tried to decide whether to follow him. Or had he? Had he wisely known that it would be dangerous for me—for both of us—if Captain Wolfe or Captain Vega should find us together?

The island had disappeared. I was wedged in between two lifeboats, uncomfortable in Mercedes' shoes, when I heard a light tread on the deck and a sailor went by, carrying a guitar and singing "eu-cu-curu," followed in a moment by Christopher Dawson. Christopher glanced up, probably attracted by my flying scarf, hesitated, but quickly passed on and would not have stopped had I not called out his name.

He turned and came back, politely took off his battered hat, and stood staring, puzzled as to who had called to him. However, only a moment went by before he spoke.

"The smile," he said. "It's you. Lucinda Benivides." He laughed, glancing at my shoes, the motheaten coat. "No wonder I didn't know you."

His hair was blowing and he put the battered hat back on and pulled it down around his ears. He laughed again.

"I see that you took my advice," he said, trying hard to hide his surprise. "I didn't think you would."

Advice? I caught my breath.

"How brave of you, Lucinda!"

He glanced down at the bag Mercedes had loaned me, which was not very big and only half full. He seemed to be at a loss for words.

"But you didn't bring many clothes," he said. "You're not planning to go back? You can't, now that you've gotten away. That would be a mistake."

The vision that had filled the night and had brought me here to the deck of the *Infanta* began to fade.

"I'll find a place for you to stay," Christopher went on. "There'll be no trouble. Now about money. You brought some? If not, I can see you through. Don Enrique gave me several thousand for my trip." He reached in his pocket. "I haven't counted it yet."

He was very businesslike as he counted the money. I had been a fool. I had made a horrible mistake. It was clear now that he hadn't asked me to run away with him. Icy fingers grasped my heart. My cheeks felt hot.

"I have money," I said angrily. "I'll go to Mount Olive. The nuns will take me in. They inherited my grandmother's ranch."

"Of course, of course, Lucinda."

I turned my back. The mainland cliffs showed clear on the horizon. Christopher was silent. The ship's clock struck twelve, eight loud bells in clusters of two. As the last notes died away, heels clicked on the deck. Captain Vega stood not far from us under a striped awning, a pearl-handled pistol strapped to his thigh.

Bowing, he said, "I have an urgent duty. Captain Wolfe has just learned from one of the maids that you are on the ship. And he has sent me to escort you to his cabin. He wishes to speak to you."

Captain Vega removed his black patent-leather cap and bowed again.

"I don't wish to be escorted," I said with a show of anger. "To Captain Wolfe's cabin or anywhere else."

"It is important," Captain Vega said in his softest voice.

I did not move. I watched a fishing boat with its outriggers spread pass under the ship's stern. A longneck cormorant circled the ship and lit on the rail not far away.

"If you will follow me, please," Vega said. He had three plump chins, not one, but he was a powerful man and dangerous, even without his weapons. "It is Captain Wolfe's fondest wish to have a word with you."

I still did not move. Christopher took my hand, about to lead me away, when Vega, with a quick, elegant twist of his body, turned, aimed one of his pistols, and fired. The cormorant fell to the deck. Two drops of blood, red as rubies, ran from its beak.

I said to Captain Vega, repeating the dead poet's fateful words, "God save thee, ancient Mariner! From the fiends, that plague thee thus!" And as I spoke I saw the death fires dancing, the water burning green and blue and white.

In one leap, I could reach the waves. Captain Vega might have seen my eyes measuring the distance from deck to sea. As quick as a striking snake, he grasped my arms. Handcuffs heavier than the ones that once had bound me to my nurse slipped over my wrists.

"This way, please," he said, leading me to the bridge deck. "You will forgive me, *señorita*. It is not my idea."

Captain Wolfe was standing at the wheel. He turned to glance at me, at the handcuffs, frowned, and turned back to scan the harbor that lay close off our bow.

"I have instructions from Don Enrique," he said, "that you are not to be allowed aboard the *Infanta* without him. I don't know whether you are aware of this or not. Probably not." When I didn't answer, he said, "It is my duty to follow instructions."

Without further words I was taken to Captain Wolfe's cabin. There, waiting for me, was his wife, Gerda. She looked very efficient in her white jacket. She had cold eyes that were almost hidden by bottle-thick glasses with a green tint to them. I never had liked her.

She nodded to Captain Vega, who removed the handcuffs and withdrew, bowing as he closed the door.

"I have a drink for you," Dr. Wolfe said, handing me a glass half full of a frothy pink liquid. "A little something to calm your nerves. This must be a truly upsetting experience . . ."

Dr. Wolfe had a heavy accent and spoke Spanish rapidly, thinking that she didn't have an accent, but I always managed to understand her. I took the glass and threw it on the floor. Making an odd sound in her throat, she backed away, opened the door, and shut it. She had never seen me angry before. I heard the key turn in the lock.

We were now inside a breakwater. On the port side of the cabin was an oval window, but it was too small for me to get my body through. I watched as we glided past anchored ships, tied up at a wharf, and Captain Vega and his squad of *pistoleros* took up positions on both sides of the gangplank.

The gold bars were carried off first and were loaded in an armored truck. The two servants left. After a long time Christopher appeared. At the foot of the gangway he put down his bag. His gaze traveled the length of the ship, then back again, seeking for some sign from me. All I need do to rest his mind, to absolve him of blame for my foolishness, to show him that I was not dying of thwarted love, was to put out my hand and wave, but I could not move.

Tears filled my eyes. Through a bright mist I saw him turn away. It was Apollo, I clearly saw, lord of Delphos, who knew all things present and future, and suddenly I was Daphne, the beautiful daughter of Peneus, who had spurned him.

Poor Apollo. Through forest and glade he had pursued me, mad with desire, gaining, gaining, so close upon me, that his breath touched my unbound hair. In panic, only in time had I thought of calling upon my father, the river god.

His magic saved me. The plea had scarcely gone from my lips than I was changing into a laurel tree. My fingers were becoming tender leaves, my toes already were roots and tendrils. In vain did Apollo lavish kisses upon my hidden flesh. I shrank from his lips. His seeking hands were repelled. His passionate cries fell upon deaf ears . . .

The vision faded. I closed the window, locked it, and pulled the drapes. I heard the gangway slide away and the big engines turn over.

9

Santiago, The
Mad Dream

A carriage was waiting on the Isla del Oro wharf as I went
down the gangplank.

On both sides stood a squad of Yaqui *pistoleros* in their
tight uniforms, obsidian eyes staring straight ahead under
black patent-leather caps. After I entered the carriage and
we started toward the castle, they mounted their horses and,
led by Captain Vega, fell in behind us.

My father was on the terrace, shading his eyes against the
setting sun. When I stepped down from the carriage, Captain Vega saluted him, as if he were delivering a dangerous
prisoner.

Don Enrique commended him for a task well done and
said to me, his voice thick with outrage, "Go to the tower,
ungrateful child. I will talk to you later tonight!"

But I did not see him that night. My dinner was brought
by a serving maid, and when I went to bed a guard was
placed at my door. The maid was an attractive woman with
lively blue-gray eyes and a fine figure, but a mute. She came
in silently and left humming to herself, never having uttered

a word, never once looking at me. I had always distrusted Alicia García and her secret ways.

Afraid of the night to come, I lay down to sleep. My cheeks burned with shame at the ridiculous fool I had been. What a ninny, what a spectacle I had made of myself!

Shame and anger, as the long night wore on, changed to pity. I reveled in pity, dozed, and awakened to it.

I saw myself as Teresa de Cabrillo y Benivides, dying of love. I was Tolstoi's abandoned little princess, Lisa, who lying in death said through waxen lips, speaking to everyone, to the world, "I love you all and have done you no harm. But what, oh what, have you done to me?"

I saw Prince Andrew gaze down upon my charming and pathetic face, my father kiss my little hands that lay quietly crossed upon my breast.

Then, as I lay there, a north wind came up and the surf began to boom against the rocks. I was Poe's beautiful Annabel Lee, and whispered to myself:

> *"A wind blew out of a cloud, chilling*
> *My beautiful Annabel Lee;*
> *So that her highborn kinsmen came*
> *And bore her away from me,*
> *To shut her up in a sepulchre*
> *In this kingdom by the sea.*
> *. . . For the moon never beams without*
> *bringing me dreams*
> *Of the beautiful Annabel Lee;*
> *And the stars never rise but I feel the bright*
> *eyes*
> *Of the beautiful Annabel Lee;*
> *And so, all the night-tide, I lie down by*
> *the side*
> *Of my darling—my darling—my life and my*
> *bride*
> *In the sepulchre there by the sea,*
> *In her tomb by the sounding sea."*

* * *

For days I was now Poe's entombed heroine, and now Anna Karenina, dying tragically beneath the wheels of a locomotive. Now Cathy Earnshaw or seduced and abandoned Clarissa Harlowe. I ate my meals alone, guarded night and day, allowed to see no one except Alicia, not even Father Martínez. I ran out of books to read. I tried to finish a story that I had started to write but I couldn't. I could only look down at the cove where I swam on sunny days and the cliff and gardens where I liked to walk in all kinds of weather.

It was during this time that curious events took place on the beach beneath my window.

The third morning of my imprisonment, at dawn, the *Infanta* sailed quietly out of the harbor and anchored in deep water some quarter of a mile from the beach. Through my glasses I made out the figure of Captain Vega, the early sun shining on his gold braid. With him were six men dressed in underwater suits and what looked to be guns wrapped in plastic.

The six men disappeared. When I caught sight of them again they were wading close to shore. There in shallow water they stopped, unsheathed their guns—machine guns—aimed at the base of the cliff, and fired.

They repeated this maneuver several times that morning and for five mornings thereafter. On the seventh morning squads of *pistoleros* set off in rubber boats, landed on the beach, and engaged in a mock battle, using guns and knives, with an imaginary foe.

Who the foe might be was a mystery. I thought of writing a note to Alicia—she was acquainted with everything that took place on the island—but her reply, judging from past experience, would be evasive. I would learn no more from her than I knew now.

The maneuvers of Captain Vega and his *pistoleros* remained a mystery until the day I left the tower, an eventful day that began with the return of Christopher Dawson from Mexico, the sudden departure of Jennifer Delaney, and ended with a bitter argument between my father and me.

Christopher arrived before noon on the *Infanta*, bringing with him a coffin similar to the one that had held the bones of Juan Rodriguez Cabrillo.

From my tower I watched it taken from the ship, reverently placed in a wagon surrounded by guards, and carried up the hill. My father and Christopher rode behind on plumed black horses. Christopher apparently was not used to horses, for he rode stiffly, holding tight to the high Spanish horn with his long legs dangling. I watched him until he was out of sight, marveling that I had ever confused him with Heathcliff or Vronsky or anyone else.

Mercedes came at noon with a tray of food, bringing news that my father had ordered the guard removed from the door and that I was free to go and come as I pleased, but not to take one step outside the castle.

I was eating lunch when Jennifer appeared, dressed in the tangerine suit and shoes she had worn the day she arrived on the island. Her hair, which had just been washed and frizzed, sparkled. Her face was flushed and she started talking before she closed the door.

"I've come to tell you goodbye," she said. "I'm leaving this afternoon. I've had fun but it's been a drill, too. It gets to you after a while. Yuck! I like your father. He's a real Spanish gentleman, but he's . . . he's"—her lips started to form the word *crazy*—"he's peculiar."

She opened the shoulder bag she was carrying. I caught a glimpse of bright metal.

"Your father must like me," she said. "He gave me this." She fumbled in the bag and fished out a bar half the size of her hand, stamped with Don Enrique's crest. "And my name too. Imagine! It's gold, isn't it?"

"Pure gold, Jennifer."

"It's very heavy," she said, and put it back in her bag. "As a guess, what do you think it's worth?"

"Ten thousand dollars," I said. Don Enrique gave one of these gold tokens to each of the women who left Isla del

Oro, so I knew its worth. "More or less, depending upon the price of gold, which varies from day to day."

I had grown to like Jennifer Delaney, though I had seen little of her. I disliked the thought of yet another woman arriving on the island to take her place. A *gringa* from the mainland, selected by my father by a strange system of his own, a woman who would stay a month, two at the most, and then, having disappointed him in some small way, would be dismissed and presented with a gold bar with her name engraved upon it, as well as a pearl choker.

Jennifer showed me her pearls. I gasped with delight, though I had seen these beautiful creations before.

I doubted that Jennifer was happy about leaving. Like most of the women, she probably entertained the hope that one day she would marry Don Enrique and become the heiress to Isla del Oro. Behind her back he called her *La Cascabalera*, "the dim-witted."

"I'll write to you as soon as I get to San Diego," she said.

I didn't bother to tell her that I received no letters from anyone except Porfirio, that they were all destroyed, at my father's request, as soon as they were delivered to the *Infanta*.

"Perhaps, Lucinda, you will come and visit me one of these days."

"Perhaps," I said.

From my window I watched the ship leave the harbor that afternoon. Jennifer waved and I waved back. The sea was calm and the sky cloudless. It was like the day I had started off on my last journey to the mainland.

Toward evening Mercedes brought word that I was to appear for dinner. I put on my prettiest gown and assumed the repentant mood that my father expected. But underneath, in the farthest corner of my soul, lay a knot of anger and foreboding.

Don Enrique was in the best of spirits. He brought a book to the table, but at no time opened its pages. Flanked by his two big staghounds, he told jokes, laughed at them, and when the talk turned serious listened to every word that was said.

Yet throughout the dinner, if our gazes met, I saw in his eyes anger that was the equal of my own.

I was finishing my dessert when Captain Vega began a discussion about some Russian machine guns that Captain Wolfe had brought up from Mexico.

I was not interested in what was said until I realized that these must be the guns Captain Vega had used in his maneuvers on the beach. At this point my father gave me a curt nod, the sign that I was excused.

I went to the music room and sat at the harpsichord. Teresa de Cabrillo y Benivides looked down upon me from her golden frame, her eyes silver in the glow of the candles, the fate we shared clearly visible, as it always was, in the sad, prophetic smile.

Impulsively I reached up and took the portrait down. I called Mercedes and had her carry it away to the storeroom, to be hidden from my eyes forever.

In the midst of a piece I was dawdling over, I heard a cry from the cavernous dining room. The single word *Santiago!* was shouted by my father, followed by a short silence, then the word was repeated by everyone at the table.

Santiago was the rallying cry of the warriors who drove the infidel Moors from Spain. It seemed strange to hear it from the throats of those at the table.

I quit dawdling. The library was open, and I wandered in to find something to read—during my imprisonment I had read everything in the tower. The heavy oak table my father worked on was cluttered as usual with objects he cherished: an ivory chessman carved from the tusk of an elephant that once had belonged to Haroun al Raschid of the *Thousand and One Nights*. A small porphyry head of an Assyrian lion. Two beautiful books from Charlemagne's library, illuminated and set with gems.

Among these familiar objects lay a colored plan. It looked to be a drawing for a mineshaft or a loading yard. Reading upside down, however, I made out the legend: *San Onofre, Uno y Dos.*

Next to the drawing was a large photograph taken from the air. It showed two round buildings, a sloping beach in front of them, and pipes that ran out into the sea with things that looked like buoys at the far ends—Father Martínez had explained it to me—an atomic plant was located at San Onofre. I had seen it often through my binoculars, lights blazing at night, steam rising from its huge domes in the daytime.

As I stood looking down at the drawing and the photograph, my father came into the room. Quickly—for I felt that they were something that I was not intended to see, that they were somehow connected with the maneuvers on the beach and the cries of *Santiago*—I turned away to search for a book.

"Here is something for you," Don Enrique said. "It's about Gaspar de Portolá."

"I read it years ago," I said. "When I was ten. It's dull."

"Yes, but the man is not. You have heard that his bones arrived this morning from Mexico. Yes. They are now in the crypt and Mr. Dawson is putting them together."

The staghounds trotted in and arranged themselves on either side of him as he sat down at the table. He put the plan and the photograph in a drawer. I seated myself across from him, a lamp between us.

Don Enrique wore a black velvet jacket and wide-bottomed velvet trousers slit up the side to show off his boots of yellow antelope hide—the costume of a *hacendado* during the days when Spain ruled California. On the finger of his left hand where he once had worn a wedding ring was a gold band set with onyx. Carved deeply in the black stone was an image of Saint James, beloved patron of the conquistadors.

"You have read this book about Portolá," he said. "What do you remember about the man who traveled two thousand leagues over snowy mountains, across the Vermilion Sea and the vast Desert of Vizcaíno, was plagued the whole journey by hostile Indians, and finally reached a village inhabited by ragged natives who ate stewed lizards, the village that was to become the great city of Los Angeles? Tell me, what do you admire most about this Portolá?"

"His bravery."

Don Enrique sniffed. "A woman's answer."

His words did not surprise me, for physically he wasn't a brave man himself. The two staghounds trailed him all day and lay by his bed at night. He slept with an Indian guard at his door and a pistol under his pillow. Nor was I surprised by his tone. He never spoke the word *woman* save in a derisive way, not for eight years, not since the night my mother left Isla del Oro.

"Think again," he said.

"Bravery," I repeated.

Don Enrique cleared his throat. "Bravery was common in those days. All the conquistadors were brave. Bravery they sucked in with their mother's milk. No, it was vision that distinguished Portolá—he saw that to hold the world Cabrillo and Vizcaíno had discovered, this marvelous new land must belong to Spain."

He got to his feet and began to pace the floor. The staghounds watched him but did not move.

"Gaspar de Portolá," he said, "was on fire with the dream of a New Spain. His dream has turned to ashes. Long ago, a hundred and fifty years ago. And yet, at this hour there live in California five million men, women, and children through whose veins flow Hispanic blood. The unconquerable blood of the conquistadors!"

Don Enrique strode to the far end of the room and returned to fix me with burning eyes.

"Portolá's dreams have faded, but they live here," he said, thumping his chest. "And soon they will live elsewhere. Five million Hispanics know little of their heritage. But they grow restless. They are angry at being people of the second class—*de clase segunda*—looked down upon by the *anglos*, underpaid, preyed upon by the unscrupulous, galled that their children attend schools where they are taught in *gringo* words the children do not understand.''

He brushed a hand through his crest of black hair. At once, like wire it sprang back. He leaned toward me, raising his voice. ''And mind you, Spain will own it again!''

His words rang out. The dogs pricked up their ears.

''The day,'' he shouted, ''the glorious day approaches. *Santiago! Viva la España!*''

The spectacular castle, the mines that poured forth riches in a golden flood, the magnificent island itself—all were his gestures of defiance, his insolent and daring answer to the hated *gringo*. This I had lived with and knew. But never had I heard a threat from him before. Nor had I imagined that secretly he harbored a dream that the flag of Spain would once more fly over the land her sons had discovered.

He poured a glass of Fundador and silently drank it. He locked the drawer where he had put the photograph and the colored plan. Suddenly the words he had just spoken, the shout of *Santiago* I had heard in the music room, the drawing and the photograph, everything came together in one awful suspicion.

''For days,'' I said, ''Captain Vega and his *pistoleros* have been running around in the cove, firing machine guns, setting off bombs, shouting *Santiago*. From this, from what you have just told me, and the plan and the picture of San Onofre I saw there on the table—from all this I fear, I am certain, you have plans that will bring ruin upon our island. Upon us all!''

He glared at me across the table. ''My plan,'' he said, ''will bring ruin only upon the *gringos*.''

Chills ran through me. ''What is it?'' I said. ''What do you plan to do?''

My father hesitated. He got up and went to the fireplace, punched the burning log with a poker, came back to the table, and sat down. He was trying to decide whether he should trust me.

"What is it?" I said. "It can't be a secret. Captain Vega and the *pistoleros* know. Captain Wolfe and Dr. Wolfe know. Whom could I tell?"

"They are ready, the Hispanics," he said, evading my question, "by the millions. California has five million Hispanics. Los Angeles alone has a million. There are millions of Hispanics in the Southwest, in Florida, in New York. They are all waiting."

"Waiting for what?"

"To be released from bondage," Don Enrique said. "The blacks also. You don't remember, you were not yet born, when they rose up and burned a town, a whole town, near Los Angeles. I count upon them to join the holy crusade."

"The Moors were black," I said, determined to voice my fears. "The Spaniards killed them by the thousands and drove them from Spain."

"Five hundred years ago."

"And the Spanish murdered most of the Indians. In the time of Columbus there were more than five hundred thousand living in the West Indies. Less than ten years later, three-fourths of them had been killed or sold into slavery."

Don Enrique scratched his head with a bony finger. "Where did you find this?"

"In a book."

"What book?"

"A book about Bartolomé de Las Casas."

"Where is this Las Casas?"

"There," I said, pointing. "In the brown leather binding."

"Get it down," he said.

I climbed the rolling ladder, pulled out the book, and handed it to him. He glanced at the title, then he walked to the fireplace and threw it into the blazing fire.

If you cannot read the truth, I said to myself, then the truth does not exist.

Don Enrique went to the farthest corner of the room and

stood there in the dark, talking to himself. Uneasily, the big gray dogs began to pace the floor.

"You were saying that millions of Hispanics were to be released from their bondage," I said. "How? By Captain Vega and his *pistoleros*? By fifty men in rubber boots?"

Stung by my scorn, Don Enrique came back to the table. The lamp was burning low and he turned it up. He opened the drawer and took out the photograph of San Onofre.

"The reactors—the atomic machines that produce electricity—are lightly guarded," he said. "There are fences and patrols on the landward approach, along the Pacific Highway. But from the sea and the beach, the main gate can be reached. By surprise at dawn. By determined men. Modern conquistadors."

I sat, unable to speak, not believing what I heard.

"Once inside the gates, once the workers are overpowered," Don Enrique said, "we will close the gates to the *anglo* world. They will not be opened until California is returned to Spain. To Spain, by discovery and conquest its rightful owner."

"What if California is not returned?" I said. "Who is to return it?"

"The governor will return it."

"What if he doesn't? If he can't return it? How can he? What then?"

"Then I shall give the signal from one of the towers that rise above us," my father said. "San Onofre will disappear in a mounting cloud of atomic dust, and with it the cities of San Diego and Los Angeles and all the cities and towns and hamlets between them."

For one long moment my heart was rent by pity. I wanted to plead with him, to cry out a warning that he would heed. I raised my hands in horror.

He saw the horror in my eyes. He left the table and came back with an envelope sealed with wax and marked with his golden crest. He shook it in my face.

"This is my will," he said, "in which you are declared

the heiress of Isla del Oro and all of its mines and to properties elsewhere. Alas, the blood of the conquistadors does not flow in your veins.''

Without another word he strode to the fireplace and tossed the envelope into the fire, beside the book that was still burning.

10

The Intruder

The woman who took Jennifer's place arrived nine days after the scene in the library.

Dorothy D'Amico looked like a statue, even in her clothes. She might have been fashioned of rosy marble. I own a picture of Botticelli's *Venus,* and that was how she appeared—like his beautiful Venus rising from the sea, her eyes still drowsy from dreams of Neptune's watery world.

She was the only woman, of all the eighteen who had appeared in the past, to be invited to dinner the first night she was on Isla del Oro. Don Enrique brought a book and his two staghounds to the table, but after no more than one long glance at Dorothy D'Amico, he told the butler to take them away.

That first night she had little to say, and this in a quiet voice, choosing to ignore my father.

She admired Captain Vega's black leather suit trimmed with silver and learned that he was born in Spain, where he had been an officer in the *Guardia Civil,* had lived on Isla del Oro for three years, and commanded an army of six hundred Tarascan and Yaqui Indians.

Opening her eyes wide, she seemed surprised at the size of his army. "Six hundred soldiers!"

"Not soldiers," Captain Vega said in his broken English. "Guardians, not soldiers."

"Your guardians are all Indians. Why Indians? They're not very bright, I understand."

Captain Vega couldn't answer the question in English, so I repeated it in Spanish and translated his reply, which was given with a great show of handsome teeth and waving of hands—he could tell a story, I think, just with his hands, without ever uttering a word.

He used Yaquis, he said, because they were the best fighters in the world—you could shoot one in the chest with a bullet and he would not drop like others, but would keep on coming at you. You would have to fire again, twice, three times, before he would give up and fall at your feet, stretching out his hand to kill you with his knife.

He used Tarascans because they were Indians of great intelligence and also good fighters—they belonged to the only tribe the fierce Aztec king Moctezuma never conquered, though he tried many times.

"And when the Spaniards conquered the Aztecs," he said, "they traveled on into the country of the Tarascans, demanded gold from the Tarascan king, and when he refused them, saying he had none, they tied him to the tail of a horse, dragged him around the village square, and at last tossed him into a fire. Even then the Tarascans would not bow their heads in submission."

Miss D'Amico seemed bored with this account, which was even longer than I have reported, but she followed it and when Captain Vega was finished asked, "Why do you have so many of these guardians? What do they guard? The gold mines?"

"Sí, las minas," Captain Vega said, lapsing into Span-

ish. *"Hay muchos ladrones y bandidos por allá."* He flourished his fork and pointed toward the mainland. *"Muchos!"*

I translated for him, saying that there were many thieves and brigands in that direction.

Captain Vega went on to recount his many exploits, some true and some imagined, while Miss D'Amico moved her head gently like a lovely flower nodding in a breeze, enthralled by what he said.

The second night was different. Don Enrique didn't bring his book or his dogs to the table, and dressed himself in his most striking *hidalgo* costume—a black velvet jacket with gold buttons, ruffled shirt, and red trousers held tight by black elastics that fit under the insteps of his shining boots. And he didn't wear the grim face he usually wore.

"How many mines do you operate?" Miss D'Amico asked him.

"Three," he said, smiling at the thought of more questions that Miss D'Amico would ask in her throaty voice. "But none of the mines at full capacity."

"The ore is smelted here? I saw the smoke."

"Smelted here into bars."

"How large are the bars?"

"Small, for easy handling. You see, gold is very heavy. A cube no larger than one foot by one foot by one foot weighs nearly a ton. The bars are no bigger than your hand."

At these facts Miss D'Amico narrowed her eyes and said, "I suppose it is safe to store gold here on the island because of Captain Vega's fine army. Across the channel in California a lot of hijacking goes on. They steal whole truckloads of money from the banks and supermarkets."

"They do many things in California that we don't do on Isla del Oro," Don Enrique said.

Dorothy D'Amico wished to know where the gold was stored.

"It is not stored," Don Enrique replied. "I ship it to the

port of Los Angeles every week, even in bad weather. Stored gold is idle gold. I prefer that it works!''

She was about to ask—or so it appeared—how many bars were shipped to Los Angeles each week. Seeing a shadow cross my father's face, she asked instead about the exciting history of Isla del Oro.

This being the subject closest to his heart, he held forth at once, while she listened enthralled, her lips slightly parted, as though in all the world the words he used had seldom been used before.

Throughout the long discourse Dr. Wolfe showed little interest. But from time to time I caught a flash from the doctor's thick glasses as her head turned to cast a quick glance at Don Enrique's new guest.

After dinner I played the harpsichord and Dorothy D'Amico sang. Her singing was not what you might expect from her speaking voice. In fact, it was somewhat strained among the high notes.

I played two pieces and then, sensing that my father wished to be alone with her, I excused myself and went to see Father Martínez, who was ill with a cold and had missed dinner both nights. In spite of his illness, I found him, his head wrapped in a shawl, standing at the telescope with the dome open.

He scurried down the ladder and began talking before he reached the floor. "Is she as beautiful as the servants report?" he wanted to know. "What does she say? Is she intelligent?"

With a real effort to be fair, mindful that he might think me jealous of Miss D'Amico, I answered his questions as truthfully as I could. I also recalled things about her that I hadn't thought of at dinner.

"She has a habit of repeating words," I said. "Don Enrique would say something like, 'We ship gold to the mainland every week.' And she would answer, 'To the mainland every week.' ''

"It's a disease. There's a name for it. What is it?" Father Martínez said, poking his brow with a finger.

"Echolalia," I said quickly, in one of my show-off moods, before he had a chance to remember. "Defined in my dictionary as 'the imitation by a child of the vocal sounds produced by others, occurring as a natural phase of childhood development.' "

Father Martínez frowned, displeased as he always was when I put my knowledge on display.

"A phase of childhood development," he said mockingly.

Not to be mocked, I replied, "Echolalia is also defined as 'the uncontrollable and immediate repetition of words spoken by another person.' "

"Echolalia annoys you?"

"She listened to what Don Enrique had to say. But I know that she was busy every moment thinking her own thoughts, whatever they were."

"It's good to have one in our midst who *does* think. The last ten or so of these women discouraged me about the world and its future."

He turned the wheel that moved the gears and the dome slid shut.

"What displeases me," he said, "is that your mother's room has been changed around to suit her taste."

"Taste? *Her* taste?"

"She's moving into . . . ."

"Into Mother's rooms?"

"She's already moved."

"When?"

"Late this afternoon."

"How does she dare? The rooms don't belong to her. They belong to my mother."

"Don't worry your head about her. She's like all the rest. Remember the second woman who came to the castle—Miss Wells, Pamela Wells? She spoke with a pretty lisp and had long, red-gold hair. Don Enrique used to gaze at her when

77

she was sitting at the harp, with her dimpled knees protruding. Then he would recall the nursery tale and say dreamily—'' Father Martínez paused, thinking.

" 'Rapunzel, Rapunzel, let down thy golden hair,' " I said to help him out.

"She was here how long?"

"Forty-five days," I said. "She'd have left sooner, except that something delayed the *Infanta* and the ship couldn't sail."

"Miss D'Amico," Father Martínez said, "will be gone in less time."

"Perhaps sooner."

Yet as I pictured a scene where Dorothy D'Amico and I looked straight at each other and I told her quietly that she had no right to my mother's rooms, I realized that I had lost my power to say anything. It had gone forever. It was I whom, at any hour, Don Enrique might banish from the island.

Father Martínez was polishing an eyepiece, blowing on the lens and wiping it with his shawl. Someone in the passageway called his name, and I recognized the voice of Christopher Dawson.

Christopher called again, this time in a louder, more excited tone, and said, "It's important!"

"If so," Father Martínez replied, "come in. If not, I'll see you in the morning."

I opened the door. Christopher rushed by, pale and disheveled. "I'd like a drink," he said. "Something strong. I've been down in the crypt, putting Portolá's bones together. They're together."

Father Martínez brought a bottle of whiskey and a glass. Christopher poured himself a large drink, finished it in one swallow, and stood staring at us.

I hadn't encountered him since his return from the mission in Mexico. He looked the same as when I saw him on the deck of the *Infanta* facing Captain Vega—his hair bushed out around his head (I wondered if he didn't comb it that way so as to resemble Erasmus or Darwin or some other famous scientist), his narrow shoulders stooped a little, and his eyes not really seeing anything or anyone.

"You are working in the crypt," Father Martínez said. "Have you found something?"

Christopher went to the door. "Come and I'll show you what I found."

Standing with his thumbs hooked into the corded belt of his gown, Father Martínez did not move.

"It's a tiresome journey," he said. "Five hundred and eleven steps from here to the crypt—I have counted them. And twice five hundred and eleven back, it seems. Besides, I enjoy a worrisome cold. Furthermore, I have little taste for surprise. Tell me, young man, what excites you so much? Are the bones of Don Gaspar de Portolá, now that you assemble them, threatening to stroll about down there in the crypt? He has a reputation for being a restless gentleman."

A trace of color had crept back into Christopher's face. He glanced at the whiskey bottle.

"You haven't come upon a hoard of Spanish doubloons?" Father Martínez asked.

"A hoard, yes," Christopher said. "But not of Spanish doubloons."

Father Martínez was suddenly suspicious. "You're not engaged in something besides the job you were hired to do?"

Christopher didn't answer. He backed away and stood at the door.

"Remember," Father Martínez said, "that you are on Isla del Oro—not the mainland—in the Castillo Santiago. And that Don Enrique de Cabrillo y Benivides is the master of the island and of the castle. I advise you to do nothing he did not instruct you to do. Nothing behind his back, lest it bode you ill."

Father Martínez was deaf to any criticism of the master of Isla del Oro.

To him Don Enrique was a devout Christian—not a follower of meek Saint Francis, rather of Saint James the warrior. But he was generous with everyone, even with the miners, though he made them carry ore strapped to their backs up wooden ladders for the good of their souls. To Father Martínez, who always reminded me of the loyal servant Sancho Panza despite his spidery looks, he was a true knight and Spanish gentleman.

The morning after my father burned his will and I learned of his mad scheme to seize the atomic plant and hold the *gringos* hostage, I had confessed my fears to Father Martínez.

"Truly mad," he said. "But nothing will come of it." He might have been Sancho speaking of his master, Don Quixote. "Once he was possessed by a scheme to corner all the world's gold. Once he invited the Pope to move his residence to Isla del Oro. As you can see, nothing came of either one."

While Father Martínez was cautioning him, Christopher had backed out of the room and was standing in the hallway.

Father Martínez called out, "Don't forget that you are here by the sufferance of Don Enrique de Cabrillo y Benivides."

Christopher motioned to me and, excusing myself, I followed him.

11

The Crystal Caskets

We went quietly past the maids' quarters. The last room in the hallway belonged to Alicia García. The door was ajar. She stood in front of a mirror combing her hair. At the sound of our steps she turned quickly and I caught a glimpse of her startled face.

When we reached the parlor on the lower floor, which the servants used during the day, Christopher told me to wait until he returned.

"I want to be sure that Don Enrique is still talking to Miss D'Amico," he said. "Don't make a noise. Don't light a candle."

I sat quietly in the dark. From minute to minute I waited for Alicia's steps on the stairs—she walked flat on her feet and made a sound that I knew well.

For several days she had been following my movements. Two days ago I had encountered her as I came up from the beach. Yesterday morning when I went to the music room she had followed me. This afternoon, while I was picking flowers in the garden, I saw her watching from a window high up in the castle.

I listened, holding my breath. I heard nothing except a machine drilling in one of the mine shafts.

Christopher was gone for what seemed a long time. As I began to wonder if something had happened to him and why I was sitting in the dark and if I would be sitting there for the rest of the night, he slipped into the room.

Grasping my hand, he led me down the corridor into the crypt, where spread out on a table were a pile of bleached bones, a helmet, a cuirass, and a rusted sword.

"I made a thorough search in Culiacán," he said, "and the hills surrounding the city. On a rumor I rode south to Guadalajara. Altogether I rode a hundred miles, but never found the grave. The bones you see on the table don't belong to Portolá. They are the bones of a Nayarit Indian I purchased along with the other things."

He paused to wipe his forehead.

"The remnants of a poor Indian and those of a conquistador," he said, "look very much alike. You can scarcely tell one from the other. It doesn't make any difference, as long as Don Enrique thinks that the bones belong to Portolá."

Surprised and yet not surprised at these cynical words, I said nothing.

He lit a candle and led me out of the crypt into a corridor black as Stygian night. "Stay close," he instructed me.

From what I had been told, I knew we were in a tunnel that curved back from the beach and wound beneath the castle. It had been dug to follow the first gold vein ever discovered on Isla del Oro. In time, when the gold pinched out, the tunnel was abandoned.

A drop of cold water fell from the roof and splashed against my cheek. The stone floor felt slippery underfoot. Our steps made hollow sounds, echoing as we went forward for nearly fifty paces and ended in a small room with an airshaft in the center of the roof. Looking up, I could see drifting clouds and patches of starry sky.

In one corner stood a two-paneled door that seemed to be new and was made of gold or bronze, I couldn't tell which. It reminded me of pictures I had seen of the doors to the Duomo in Florence, which everyone thought were bronze but centuries later, when they were cleaned and polished, turned out to be gold.

With effort Christopher swung the panels aside, revealing a small vestibule and in the far wall another door, this one smaller and clearly made of gold. He opened the door and, snuffing out his candles, moved aside for me to pass.

I took a step, one short step, and halted. Before me stretched a vast room whose walls and floor and ceiling were made of black marble. It was lit by dozens of the big votive candles that were made to burn for weeks.

"I stood here, too," Christopher said, "and couldn't move. Walk in."

The smell of incense came out of the room, the same heavy odor that I had smelled in the crypt. I was blinded by the glitter of candles on the black marble. When my vision cleared I stepped across the threshold.

In the center of the chamber, arranged in an orderly way, with side aisles between, was a row of what seemed to be glass cases, like ones I had seen pictures of, standing at shoulder height for better viewing.

I approached the first case, Christopher close behind me. I saw before I had gone far that it was made not of ordinary glass, but of the finest crystal. Then, to my amazement, I saw that it was not a museum case, as I had thought, but a casket and that inside the casket lay a woman.

I must have screamed, for the next thing I remember was that Christopher had his hand clamped tight over my mouth. I was standing at the head of the coffin, looking down upon the face of the first *gringa* who ever came to Isla del Oro.

It was the face of Margaret Drew—her rosebud mouth, the nostrils that gently flared, the small ears that nestled close to her head, her broad brow, and the long lashes curving down over her closed eyes.

She was dressed in a white silk blouse and skirt that I remembered. She had white slippers on her feet—one of the heels was run down a little on the side—and sheer blue stockings.

At the foot of the coffin, set deep in the crystal, was a gold bar stamped with the name Margaret Drew—the same gold bar Don Enrique had given her as a token on the day she left Isla del Oro.

I turned to Christopher. We stared at each other.

"There's no need for you to go on," he said. "There are seventeen more. The last is Jennifer Delaney."

"But I saw Jennifer leave the island," I said. "I was in the tower when the *Infanta* sailed. I saw her standing at the rail. She waved to me and in answer I waved back. She can't be here."

"She is," Christopher said. "There at the far end of the room. The last one."

I hurried along the row, past seventeen coffins. At the eighteenth I stopped and looked down at the gold bar, then at the woman beneath the crystal glass. It was Jennifer Delaney, dressed in the tangerine suit she wore the day I saw her last.

I was struck by a sudden fear. It was possible that my mother lay here amidst this horde of women. I ran back, glancing through the crystal lids.

It wasn't necessary to read the inscriptions, for I remembered the faces—Helen Barnes, who looked like a Raphael madonna, and Beth Donaldson and her twin sister, Bernadine, and Linda, the girl who wrote poetry.

Near the end of the long row I came upon a face framed in ringlets of golden hair.

For a moment, a frightful moment, I thought that it was my mother's face. Then I saw that it was Kimberley Wood, who at first glance looked like my mother, lying there peacefully with her pale hands folded. I reached the end. My mother was not in the room.

Christopher, who had followed me, said, "Could this be the work of your father? Or Captain Wolfe? Who? You're sure about Jennifer waving from the ship? You saw her?"

"I am positive."

"Then the ship must have turned back when it was out of sight and put her ashore on some part of the island, where she was picked up and brought here. Possibly by Captain Vega."

I couldn't get my thoughts together. All I could say was, "Why?"

Christopher ignored me. "The bodies were embalmed by an artist, by someone who has had experience. Who could it be? I wonder. Alicia García? Yesterday while I was working in the crypt she came by, disappeared, then turned but didn't come back. Out of curiosity I went to investigate. This is what I found."

"Why didn't she lock the door?"

"For some reason they don't have locks."

An explosion from one of the mine shafts sent a tremor rippling through the floor. Candles dipped and fluttered. Shadows shifted along the crystal coffins and changed their shapes. Echoes lingered for a while. Then a deep and menacing silence fell upon the room.

"This is not a museum," Christopher said. "Visitors are not welcome here." His face had a sickly look in the amber light.

"Not us, especially," I said.

We closed the doors behind us, the small gold door and the one with the two panels. Quietly we made our way back along the tunnel and through the crypt to the maids' parlor. Here in the darkness, speechless, we parted.

I climbed the servants' stairs and as I turned down the corridor toward Alicia's room, I heard the faintest of sounds. A wind had sprung up and at first I thought that it was what I heard. But as I passed her door, which was closed, I realized that the sounds came from her room. She was humming, as she did most of the time, a plaintive sound under her breath, like the wind itself.

12

Fatal Words

Soon after midnight a *chubasco* blew in from the south, wind with rain that built up a running surf and a heavy sea. At dawn I went to Mercedes' room.

She was asleep but I awakened her. She lit a candle, staggered back to bed, and stared at me as I described the crypt and what I had seen. I believe at first she thought that I was walking in my sleep.

"You know nothing about the crypt?" I said.

She opened her mouth to speak. No words came out.

"The servants haven't said anything?"

Mercedes shook her head. Her mouth was still open.

"Alicia? Could she know something? Christopher has seen her flitting around the crypt while he was at work. Could it be Villaverde?"

Mercedes recovered her voice. "Let me think. Yes, tonight—perhaps it doesn't mean anything—tonight before dinner, I caught sight of Alicia trotting up the stairs from the storeroom. She was carrying a basket of the big votive candles. I was in the kitchen, and when she saw me she whirled around and went down the stairs.''

"The servants," I said, "are busy all day with candles, gathering up the old ones, putting new ones in the sconces.''

"Candles are done in the morning," Mercedes said. "Always in the morning. I see to it that they're done right after breakfast.''

"Alicia might have been on her way to the crypt when you saw her. She's just the one among all the servants who would like such a task and attend to it well.''

Mercedes had turned the color of the bedsheet she was clutching to her chest. "Heavens," she said, "what's to be done? Have you told Father Martínez? He's the only one on Isla del Oro who has any influence with your father.''

"It would do no good," I said. "He wouldn't believe a word of it.''

"Take him down there and show him the crypt.''

I explained how he had refused to go with Christopher. "Father Martínez gave him a sharp lecture about Castillo Santiago and wouldn't budge.''

"He must have known that something was wrong, from the excited way you say Christopher carried on.''

"I doubt it.''

"If you took the old man by the arm," Mercedes said, "down the stairs, through the tunnel, into the marble chamber and showed him the coffins, would he believe what he saw?''

"I doubt that also. Whatever he saw, Don Enrique couldn't be a party to it. To Father Martínez, my father is a Spanish gentleman, a *hidalgo*—a strict and unbending follower of the code.''

"You are full of doubts, *señorita*, but you don't doubt that you saw a chamber down at the end of the tunnel where there are eighteen crystal coffins in a row and black marble walls that shine in the candlelight.''

Mercedes paused. Her voice began to tremble. "You

weren't dreaming, were you? You weren't walking in your sleep, Lucinda?''

''I saw it. It is there at the end of the dark tunnel. Just as I described it.''

''Father Martínez should be told.''

''What can he do? Even though he sees it with his own eyes. Even though he believes what he sees?''

''He will tell Don Enrique.''

''What if Don Enrique knows? What if Don Enrique built the chamber? What if Don Enrique himself filled the coffins?''

''Someone else could have killed them,'' Mercedes said.

''Who?'' I said. ''And for what reason?''

''You should tell Father Martínez,'' she insisted.

''It would do no good. He'll call everyone to the church and threaten hellfire and damnation. Those who did this will listen politely and go on their way.''

''Everyone on the island will know about it, then.''

''Everyone on the island is a prisoner, like you and me. Like Father Martínez himself. He more than any of us, because he loves Don Enrique.''

Mercedes shivered. She pulled the sheet tight around her. Only her face showed, stark white and strained.

''Your mother is not down there?'' she said.

''No, I looked.''

''You're certain?''

''She can't possibly be there. I saw her leave the castle that night. She ran out on the terrace and fled. I saw her.''

Beneath the sheet Mercedes crossed herself. One finger stole out to touch her lips and linger there.

''The servants are at it,'' she said. ''They're talking about your mother again. They think she's behind the wall.''

''They have thought that for a long time. On and off,'' I said, feeling the pain I always felt at this horrible thought.

''Forgive me, but now more than ever. Since the day Cabrillo's bones were brought here.''

"Tell the servants," I said angrily, "tell each of them so they will all understand it, that they will be punished . . ."

I left Mercedes rigid in her bed, still clutching the sheet to her thin chest, and went to the kitchen in the hope of finding Christopher. A *gringo*, he always took his meals with the servants in the parlor where I had waited for him the previous night. He had already eaten his breakfast, according to the cook, and had gone to work on the bones he had brought from Mexico.

I didn't dare follow him to the crypt. I went back to my tower and barred the door, fearful that Don Enrique might have learned from Alicia, from someone, that I had been in the chamber only hours before and would come to threaten me.

While I was in Mercedes' room, the rain had stopped. The sky was clear, except to the east, where a cloud of blue-gray smog, shaped like a scimitar, curved out from the mainland. In the cove, Captain Vega and his band of *pistoleros* were holding maneuvers again, swimming in from the *Infanta*, rowing shoreward in their rubber boats, blasting away with machine guns at targets set up against the cliff.

At targets similar to those they would encounter in their attack upon San Onofre?

I didn't see Christopher until the next evening, when the bones he had carefully assembled and flanked with helmet, cuirass, and sword were put to rest. The ceremony was the same as the one for Admiral Cabrillo, attended by all the important people of the island, presided over by Father Martínez.

There wasn't the least sign from Don Enrique that he had learned that Christopher and I had stood in the chamber he had built and peopled with the *gringas* who had come to Isla del Oro. He treated me, as he had since the night he burned his will, with elaborate courtesy.

There were the same songs as before and a gloomy procession down the winding stairs. Dorothy D'Amico seemed fascinated with everything. She would have been fascinated even more had she known that the bones she stood beside, her white shoulders gleaming in the candlelight, did not belong to Gaspar de Portolá. That not far away at the end of a dark tunnel was a chamber unlike any she had ever seen or imagined. And that one day she herself might repose there.

Afterward a reception was held in the drawing room, and Don Enrique announced to his guests that the next great Spaniard to be brought to Isla del Oro and given burial was Junípero Serra.

"Father Serra," he explained to those who had never heard of the father (and there were many), "is the indomitable Franciscan who followed in the steps of Gaspar de Portolá. This man, who limped on a bad leg that would never heal, though it was treated often with a burning iron, journeyed on foot, always on foot, more than a thousand leagues from Mexico City to the coast of California. There he began founding missions, one after another, a day's horseback ride between them, until a chain of missions reached from San Diego in the south to San Francisco in the north."

When he had finished with this talk, I overheard Miss D'Amico conversing with him about Father Serra.

"A great man," she said, "who sought the fickle hand of martyrdom and failed to find it. I am familiar with his life. I know that he is buried in the Mission San Carlos at Carmel. Tell me, *hidalgo*"—she liked to use this aristocratic title when addressing him—"how do you propose to bring him here to Isla del Oro? You can't have someone just walk in and seize his coffin. Wouldn't you and your men be stopped by the police and arrested for thievery?"

The two moved away, out of my hearing. I didn't hear Don Enrique's reply to this tactless remark. But I caught a glimpse of his face and I can truthfully say that it had a deep look of sadness. Then, after a moment, the sadness was gone and his eyes suddenly smoldered with a strange, inhuman light. Don Enrique de Cabrillo y Benivides, a common thief!

There were requests for me to perform on the harpsichord, and I obliged. Captain Vega and his wife and several others clustered around me, among them Christopher Dawson. I hadn't said a word to him since the night before last when we had parted in silence.

"I had a talk yesterday with your father," he said, speaking in English, which none of the Spaniards around us understood. "He planned to send me north tomorrow on the Serra project. Just now, he changed his mind. He thinks it better to wait a week or so."

At Captain Vega's request I was playing an Andalusian air, which he was singing in his thin tenor voice. It was difficult to play and think at the same time.

"Miss D'Amico criticized him tonight about the Serra thing," I said. "She may have given him a scare, saying that he might be arrested as a thief."

"No, he believes that he's above the reach of *gringo* law, absolutely. He's moved the Serra project ahead to make it fit in with the attack on . . ." Christopher hesitated to use the word *San Onofre* and decided to say instead, " . . . on the plant across the channel. He thinks, I suppose, that there'll be so much confusion that no one would notice what's happening to Serra."

Captain Vega quit singing for a moment. *"Serra,"* he said, *"era un hombre mucho macho."*

"I also think," Christopher said, "that he no longer trusts me to leave the island. He knows that I would alert the authorities, the Coast Guard, and the police."

"He's found out that we discovered the chamber?"

"I am not sure he didn't want us to."

As I finished the Andalusian piece everyone clapped their hands and the wife of Don Q, the superintendent of the mines, asked me to play "Espinita."

I hadn't played this tune for a long time, but I did my best, while Captain Vega hummed again and Don Q's wife joined him, singing the words.

"We know—" I said, "we suppose that my father gave

the orders for the murders. But who did the killing and who embalmed the corpses?''

"The embalming is artful. Not the work of an amateur. The only person on Isla del Oro who has this skill is G. W.,'' Christopher said, referring to Gerda Wolfe, not calling her by name for just then she was standing beside him. "And she's as cold-blooded as a barracuda.''

I lost the tune of "The Little Thorn" and had to start over.

"What puzzles me is how and where they were killed,'' Christopher said. "You told me that you saw Miss J. leave the island.''

"She stood at the rail and waved her scarf. I saw her,'' I said, speaking quietly in time with the music. "I waved back at her until she was out of sight.''

"Did the ship go east, south, or north?''

"Straight east for a while. Then to the north and out of sight.''

I finished "Espinita.'' Captain Vega asked for "Rancho Grande,'' but before I began, I said to Christopher, "She was going to L.A., so I thought it odd when the ship turned north. And it seems odd to me now. What if the ship landed at the isthmus, three leagues north of here, with J. alive or dead?''

"It would mean that the man in charge of the ship, as well as his wife, is an accomplice of your father.''

"As well as V. He and his men command every foot of the shoreline. There are three for us to deal with. Three we know of.''

Christopher took a deep breath. "I haven't told you. I haven't had a chance. I went back to the chamber early this morning. An empty coffin has been moved into the chamber, the nineteenth.''

I started on the raucous "Rancho Grande,'' which sounds terrible on a harpsichord and most any time. Captain Vega clapped, stomped his booted feet, and gave a yelp at the finish, "Ayee!''

Christopher said, "Don Enrique has been watching us. He's coming now."

"*Now*," Captain Vega said, making it sound like *naa*, "what does *now* mean?"

"It means *ahora*," I said.

"Don Enrique now," he said with a sly smile, pretending to speak English.

Don Enrique pushed him to one side. Whereupon Captain Vega carefully bowed himself away and everyone followed him.

My father said, "You have become very accomplished. You play and you converse, both at the same time. The conversation was long and quite earnest. Does something trouble you?"

"Nothing."

"You're certain?"

I stood up and faced him. He sought to stare me down, to reach my innermost thoughts, my tattered soul. For a moment I was Trilby O'Ferral facing Svengali. For a moment I saw Svengali as his creator had described him, ". . . thick, heavy, languid, lustreless black hair fell down behind his ears . . . He had bold, brilliant black eyes, with long, heavy lids, a thin, sallow face."

Trilby O'Ferral had never escaped from that mysterious and turbulent stranger until the day of his death.

The vision faded.

My father said, "Nothing troubles you?"

I closed the keyboard and walked to the door. Then I turned to look at the portrait of Teresa de Benivides. I had forgotten that it was hidden away.

"Nothing," I said. "*Nada.*"

Miss D'Amico was talking to Christopher Dawson as I left the drawing room. She looked ravishing in her sequined gown, which covered all of her front but little of her back.

I am certain she hadn't the least suspicion that she had offended Don Enrique. She hadn't seen his eyes glitter when she asked, of his plan to seize Serra's remains, "Wouldn't you and your men be stopped by the police and arrested for thievery?''

Like all of the others—like Jennifer Delaney, who played rock music, like Nancy Anne Walker, who spoke endlessly of liberating women from the cruel domination of men, like Cynthia Storm, who loved birds and spent days and nights trying to capture the quetzal that was still loose on the island, like all the other women—Dorothy had disappointed him.

Besides—and this thought had just struck me while I sat at the harpsichord talking to Christopher Dawson—she was a *gringa*. Like all the rest, Dorothy was one of the race that had humiliated Spain, a race upon whom my father had sworn everlasting revenge.

13

The Nineteenth

I climbed the stairs as though I were being pursued, feeling a cold hand on my back.

I reached the tower, opened the door, and barred it behind me, standing against the barred door to catch my breath. I went to the window, the little porthole that opened upon a world of sky and sea and the far-off shore of the mainland.

I looked out into the dark night of scattered stars and tumbling clouds. Solemnly, seeing my father's eyes staring down at me, his lips drawn thin and his jaw set in one last effort to hold me captive, I said aloud to him in a voice that did not tremble, "The spell is broken. It is broken forever."

I heard the *Infanta*'s bell strike the hour. One of Captain Vega's speedboats went by on its nightly patrol, leaving a trail of phosphorescence. Far down on the horizon the lights at San Onofre showed bright against a black sky.

A short time later I heard Dorothy D'Amico's door open and close. I waited a moment, then went down the hallway to her rooms, the rooms my mother had lived in once. I stood at the door for what might have been one minute or five, and tried to find the courage to knock.

I must have made a sound, for suddenly she was there in the doorway. She didn't seem surprised. I even had the feeling, as she stepped aside and smiled, that she had expected me.

I saw that she was using the sitting room for more than a place to sit. On the desk a vase was filled not with flowers but with pencils; notebooks and a fat dictionary cluttered the desk. The wastebasket over-flowed with sheets that had been crumpled and thrown away.

"You have been here before," Miss D'Amico said. "You probably have a favorite chair. Which? This is the one I like. It's French. I like the way the legs curve, and the seat invites one to sit down. It must be old."

"It is," I said. "It came from the palace of Louis the Fourteenth."

Through the hallway that joined the sitting room to my mother's bedroom I caught a glimpse of the bed she had slept in. It looked unused, exactly the same as the day she left. The three pillows rested stiffly against the headboard. The coverlet had the same deep folds. Dorothy D'Amico, for whatever reason, hadn't used it.

I sat down, but not in Louis XIV's chair, which always appeared ready to collapse.

"It has an expensive look," Miss D'Amico said.

"Yes," I said, remembering what the chair had cost, that the extravagant price had led my mother to raise her eyebrows—her way of showing displeasure when Don Enrique paid twice what something was worth.

At the far end of the bedroom I could see the alcove, the gold-knobbed drawers on both sides, and beyond, in the shadows, the gray stone wall.

Miss D'Amico was saying, "I haven't had a chance to talk to you. How do you spend your time? Studying? Reading?" She went to the desk, turned over a sheet of paper that had a few lines of writing on it, and sat down again. Was she hiding what she had written? "There's so little for a girl of your age to do here on the island."

She emphasized the word *girl*—or at least I thought she did.

"You read a lot," she continued. "A book every day, I hear."

"At least. Sometimes more."

"What do you read, Spanish books?"

"No, mostly Dickens and Thackeray and Darwin and Shakespeare."

"English writers."

"French, too. Stendhal. Molière. Dumas. Balzac, Balzac especially. And the Russians."

"No American writers?"

"Lots of them," I said. "Longfellow and Emerson and Herman Melville. I've read about his great white whale three times. I've never seen a white one, but the gray whales go past the castle in January and February. They come from the north, the Aleutians, and swim south to Baja California to have their calves. Then they go back in the spring. And I have read all of Whittier and Edgar Allan Poe."

"Emily Dickinson?"

"She's one of my favorites."

"And mine. A sweet, rebellious spirit." Then she thought for a moment and said:

> *"Rowing in Eden—Ah! the Sea!*
> *Might I not moor tonight in thee."*

I said:

> *"There is no Frigate like a Book*
> *To take us lands away*
> *Nor any Coursers like a Page*
> *Of prancing Poetry."*

* * *

And then Dorothy said:

> *"Love's stricken "why"*
> *Is all that love can speak—*
> *Built of but just a syllable*
> *The biggest hearts that break."*

The word was "hugest hearts" and not "biggest hearts," but I didn't correct her. I said:

> *"Where ships of purple—gently toss—*
> *On seas of daffodil—*
> *Fantastic sailors—mingle—*
> *And then—the wharf is still!"*

"You don't know any of the modern writers?" Dorothy said.

I shook my head, embarrassed.

"Then I'll make a list for you. Imagine reading *The Great Gatsby*. Or *The Good Soldier*. Or *Death Comes for the Archbishop*. Or *An American Tragedy*. The list will take a little time. I'll start on it tomorrow."

"There's no point in making a list," I said. "I'm not allowed to read new books."

"A rule of Castillo Santiago?"

"A law," I said, still embarrassed, glancing at my mother's desk, cluttered now with papers. "The servants tell me that you spend a lot of your time writing. Are you writing about Isla del Oro?"

Dorothy D'Amico was sitting on the French chair with her legs crossed at the ankles. She uncrossed them and sat up straight.

"The island has a dramatic history," she said, not answering my question. "The early explorers, Juan Cabrillo and Portolá, the conquistadors, the family feuds, the gold mines, Castillo Santiago, which cost fifteen million dollars to build and half as much to furnish."

All this I saw in a brief flood of memories—my ancestors, the fabled island, the mysterious castle that many thought was haunted, my lonely life as a princess and a prisoner. All returned. Then it quickly vanished. What remained was the awful vision of the marble-lined chamber and the row of crystal coffins. The gray stone wall nearby.

"You've lived a part of this story," Dorothy D'Amico said. "Why don't you write about it?"

"Because no one would believe what I wrote."

"Readers like to believe the unbelievable," she said.

"I wouldn't think of writing it, even if I could."

Miss D'Amico seemed relieved. She smiled, showing teeth as perfect as pearls in a necklace. How beautiful she looked in her fuchsia gown! She brushed back her hair lightly with both hands.

"You could write something less ambitious," she said. "Simpler than the story of Isla del Oro. Something for children. I would be pleased to help you."

"I've tried. But my writing always ends up sounding like the last book I've read."

She went to the desk and took a cigarette with a violet-colored mouthpiece from the drawer.

"I suppose you know that your father doesn't approve of smoking," she said, lighting the cigarette.

"And of other things, too."

"But he's a dear. He does so many lovely things."

She drew cigarette smoke deep into her chest, as Jennifer did, and let it out through her nostrils in two thin, opalescent streams of smoke, like those a dainty dragon might make.

"I wish he would allow you more freedom," she said. "Perhaps we can go to Los Angeles sometime. Just the two of us. I'll ask."

There were no ashes on the tip of her cigarette—she had only been smoking for a moment or two—but she tapped it into the ashtray nonetheless. She did it three times. She had strong fingers and the taps made a loud noise in the quiet room. Her thoughts were off somewhere, but she smiled again to let me know that she hadn't forgotten I was still there.

The brutal need came to me as I sat admiring the elegant way she toyed with her cigarette, abruptly out of a dark corner of my heart, the darkest of all, the need to let her know that the chair she sat upon and the rooms she had used since she appeared on Isla del Oro belonged to my mother and that she was an intruder.

Miss D'Amico had crushed out her cigarette and was lighting another. She stood looking at me, at my face that felt drained of blood.

"Can you see," I asked her, "do you see the stone wall beyond the bedroom? There at the far end of the alcove?"

"Yes. I see it every day and I think it's very ugly. I have asked Don Enrique to tear it down or cover it with wallpaper. A pastoral scene, perhaps. Or a view of the Seine and Notre Dame."

"What did he say?"

"That he'd attend to it."

"When?"

"At once. As soon as he's finished with a very important project. Something he calls *Santiago*. Something you wouldn't know because he doesn't confide in you."

"Do *you* know what he means by *Santiago*?"

"Nothing, except that he's been talking about it a lot and brought it up tonight at dinner. *Santiago* must have something to do with the Serra thing. It gives me the cold creeps," she said, drawing an imaginary shawl around her bare shoulders. "The whole idea . . . bringing Serra's bones here and . . ."

Miss D'Amico was treating me like a child. I resented it.

"He has two different ideas," I said. "Serra has nothing to do with either one, Miss D'Amico."

"Dorothy," she corrected me.

"*Santiago* is a scheme to seize an atomic plant," I said.

Miss D'Amico was squinting at me through a curtain of

cigarette smoke. She waved it away with a slow movement of her hand. "Atomic plant?" she said. "Where?"

I would have said no more, leaving her in the dark, but her manner was very condescending.

"Less than thirty miles away," I said. "On the mainland. You can see it from my window."

"Don Enrique plans to seize an atomic plant? What then? What will he do with it?"

"Hold it for ransom," I said. "As hostage."

"Really?" she said, repeating the same word several times while I was explaining to her my father's dream—the conquest of California and its return to the motherland.

"Impossible!" she said when I had finished. "You're making this up. You can't be serious."

"I *am* serious," I said.

She must have thought that I was either a liar or a disturbed adolescent for she abruptly changed the subject.

"We'll give a program some night," she said. "On the terrace, now that the weather is pleasant. You play with great feeling for one so young."

"The 'Serra thing,' as you call it, Miss D'Amico, is timed to take place at that hour . . . at the same hour as the attack upon the atomic plant. In that way, with all the excitement—people running around not knowing whether they'll be alive the next moment or dead—it won't be noticed."

She stared at me.

"Serra and *Santiago* will be undertaken because my father's life and fortunes were pledged to them long ago," I said. "They both are doomed to fail, but people may die by the thousands."

She continued to stare at me now, as if she were certain that a streak of madness ran through the veins of the Benivides family and that I, alas, had inherited it.

"We may die among the thousands," I said. "Both of us."

Miss D'Amico put out her cigarette, though she hadn't

smoked half of it. Her mouth curled in a small, polite yawn. "I'm sorry," she said. "It's been a long day for me. I didn't sleep well last night."

Nor will you sleep well tonight, I was tempted to say.

I had come to tell her that behind the gray stone wall she found so ugly, which had been erected by Don Enrique and which he had promised to tear down sometime and change to suit her tastes, that behind the ugly gray wall, if the servants' gossip was true, there lay two bodies—the body of my mother and the body of a man, her lover.

But the moment was not right. I would only add to her conviction that she had stumbled into the midst of an insane family.

"You will need a wrap," I said, getting to my feet. "It is very cold where we're going. And a pair of walking shoes, the stones are uneven."

She picked up a third cigarette, put it in her mouth, but didn't light it. She was uncertain about what I had said.

"We're going," I said, "to a place you have never seen."

Something in my voice caught her attention, stirred her, for without a word she threw on a sweater and followed me out of the room. Alicia's door was closed, but a thread of light shone at the threshold.

We went down the winding stairs, through the crypt, and along the dark passageway, each carrying a hooded candle. There was a faint odor of smoke in the tunnel and the first door and the second were ajar. For a moment I thought that someone had been there just before us—Alicia or Villaverde?—but when we entered the burial chamber we found it deserted.

In their deep niches, the votive candles were new and all were burning. They cast a mellow light upon the crystal caskets. Bouquets of fresh flowers, arranged tastefully here and there, gave off a cloying odor.

Dorothy D'Amico was half through the doorway, standing motionless, blinded by the light that leaped from the marble walls and danced upon the crystal.

"Come," I said, taking her ice-cold hand and leading her to the first of the caskets. "This is Margaret Helen Drew. She was the first of the women who came to the island."

Miss D'Amico gazed quickly at the pretty face, at the rosebud mouth, the long, curving lashes. She didn't move or speak or make a sound. Her skin, no longer the rosy white of marble, was the color of chalk.

I led her down the row of caskets, calling each woman by name, saying something about each. Only now, in place of eighteen, I counted nineteen caskets. Since the night Christopher and I were here another had been added, identical to the others, except—I saw with horror—that this one was different.

Dorothy D'Amico stood rigid, clasping the candle to her breast. Then she made an odd sound and uttered her first words. "There's no one in it," she gasped, staring down through the crystal lid at a bed of tufted silk and tassels. "It's empty!"

My tongue was a dry leaf. "Empty," I said under my breath, out of pity keeping the thought to myself: Empty now, but not for long.

Suddenly, as we stood there in silence, I heard a stirring, a rustle of something moving slowly along the wall behind us. I shielded my eyes from the glitter of the crystal caskets.

A shape was emerging from the shadows, a dark gliding shape, its lineaments too dim to make out. Then the shape came into a square of light cast down by a votive candle.

The serpent had a blunt nose and eyes like black diamonds. Its tongue swept from side to side as if it were tasting the perfumed air. I recognized it from the pointed scales arranged in patterns of salmon pink and jet black— from the description I had once read. We were confronted by a serpent that had escaped from the wrecked ship, one of the deadly bushmasters.

The serpent lowered its head, raised it again, then stopped a few paces away and gathered itself.

It made no sound while it did this. And an instant later, remembering that I had read in the letter from the zoo that the bushmaster did not attack unless provoked, we moved away, one cautious step at a time.

The serpent placed there to guard the crystal chamber did not follow us.

14

Eve's Friend,
the Serpent

At dawn a heavy mist hid Encantada Cove, the cliff, the beach, and the surf, yet I clearly heard the ship's anchor chain run out and, rising like murky bubbles through the mist, the shrill commands of Captain Vega.

"*Ratones,*" he shouted. "*Hijos de ratones,* sons of rats. You do not descend backward, clambering like a chicken." Then a curse, followed by "*Monos locos,* crazy monkeys, I inform you for the tenth time to feather the oars." Then the rattle of machine guns and the thud of bullets. I couldn't see Captain Vaga, but he was there in the cove, resplendent in his glossy braid, starting another day of practice for the assault upon San Onofre.

Toward noon the maneuvers shifted to the castle grounds. Men climbed the cliff at the head of the cove, pistols in hand and grenades strapped to their waists. The enemy, the *gringos,* ran out from a secret passage and met them as they reached the terrace. There was thunderous noise and bullets flew everywhere, but only a few *pistoleros* were injured in the mock battle. Don Enrique watched from one of the towers.

Flying the red and gold flag of ancient Spain, the *Infanta* sailed that night for the mainland. She returned at dusk two days later, carrying as passengers dozens of strange men and strange women. Shortly before they arrived at the castle, Don Enrique summoned me to the library.

Attired in one of his *hidalgo* costumes, his hair oiled and combed in *furioso* style, seated in the library, a map spread out before him, and the two staghounds crouched on either side of his chair, he greeted me with an elegant sweep of his hand, motioning me to a chair.

"The people you will meet tonight," he said, "I have never seen before. They are known to me by name only. They are all *gringos,* but I expect you to be courteous. Reserved but courteous in the true Benivides tradition. Do you understand?"

"Yes, courteous yet distant."

"You have seen few people from the mainland. No men, as I recall."

"Only women," I said without thinking.

Don Enrique's expression did not change. "Yes, only *gringas,*" he said. "And a poor lot as I recall. Those you meet tonight will be different. All are leaders. They are the heads of religious and political movements and so-called radicals. They will help me when the right moment comes."

"What moment?" I said, though I knew well what he meant. "Not San Onofre. Not *Santiago.*"

From far back in their deep sockets his eyes caught the lamplight. Two small glints, sharp as nails, were fixed upon me.

"Santiago, sí," he cried.

The big staghounds stirred, glanced at him, then at me, raised their muzzles to sniff. He leaned across the table and lowered his voice.

"You are to say nothing about San Onofre," he said. "Nothing. Not tonight. Not to anyone. Is this understood?"

"Yes, but I will say now to you, Father, that it will bring ruin upon us all. I can't understand how . . ."

"I puzzle you," he broke in. "I cause you distress." He clasped his hands in a humble gesture. "You have read Machiavelli. Then you must know that he is often my guide and mentor. Knowing this, you should know me."

I took up his challenge. "There are two ways of contesting," I said, quoting his master. "The one by law, the other by force. The first method is proper to men, the second to beasts."

"You select words with great care," my father said. "Machiavelli also says that when the first method is not sufficient, it becomes necessary to have recourse to the second. To beastly actions, Lucinda. To the actions I am forced to take."

He smiled a half-smile of satisfaction. He seemed pleased that he had branded himself as a beast and thus forestalled my criticism. Rising, he went to the window and glanced down at the terrace, where colored lights were being strung for the evening and wisps of smoke from Captain Vega's late maneuvers still hung in the air.

When he came back to the table I quoted to him the words of Montaigne, a writer he despised. "Those who give the first shock to the state are apt to be the first ones swallowed up in its ruins."

His smile faded. "Ruin already exists," he said. "More is not possible." He held up his hand to end the argument. He rolled the map and put it away. He called Villaverde to trim the guttering lamp.

When the servant had left, he said casually, as if speaking of some incident he thought mildly interesting, "A message comes to me that you have been a visitor to . . ." He paused, choosing the word he wanted. "To the pantheon."

I was astounded to hear the place mentioned at all. For a moment I could think of nothing to say. Then, as casually as he had spoken, not to display my knowledge but to gain time to think, I said, *"Pantheon* is not correct. The *Panthéon* is a national monument in Paris, a sepulcher for famous Frenchmen. *Pantheon,* without the acute accent, is the domed temple in Rome built by Hadrian in the years 120–124 and used as a public building to contain the tombs or memorials of the illustrious dead.''

My words began to tremble—I trembled all over.

Don Enrique said, *"Pantheon,* as I use the word, is correct. By definition it means a temple dedicated to gods or to goddesses. In this case, my dear, to neither. To women who proved all too mortal. I prayed that with Miss D'Amico I had found a goddess at last, at last.''

The staghounds, aroused by sounds on the terrace, trotted to the window. He called them back, patting the head of each one, and leaned across the table to take my hands in his. Cold, they held mine in a tight grip.

''The pantheon is always open to you,'' he said. ''Be it night or day, you are always welcome there. But I warn you, it is guarded by a watchful serpent.''

His eyes smoldered. His grip tightened on my hands.

''Eden's garden,'' he said, ''was also guarded by a serpent. A cunning beast. When Eve paid heed to its blandishments, evil entered the world. Thus woman became the source of many evils. Yet in pure innocence and need I keep searching for one without evil. Alas, my search has failed. Always doomed to fail? Forever?''

He sat with his thin face thrust forward. The lamplight shone on his hollow cheeks and the deep hollows in his temples.

At this moment, as I met his gaze, all of the suspicions that had built up in me during the past weeks suddenly came together in one unshakable truth. My father, Don Enrique de Cabrillo y Benivides, was deranged.

Across the table, with his eyes fixed upon me, sat a madman. Sat insane Torquemade, Inquisitor General of all Aragon, organizer of the Spanish Inquisition, who put hundreds to death for their lack of faith. Sat Gilles de Rais, one of France's richest nobles, who killed a thousand children, one by one, to satisfy his ungodly tastes.

But what could I say to a madman, to a madman who was

my father? What words would comfort him, and should he be comforted? How could I stop his headlong rush toward disaster?

"You are to say nothing," he said. "Not a word to our *anglo* guests about the secrets we share. And you are not to discuss them with Dorothy D'Amico, with whom, against my wishes, you have become friendly. Who came here, I have learned, to write a story about Isla del Oro. What she has written—some hundred pages of lies and conjectures—I have seized. Alicia burned them this morning." He still held my hands in an unyielding grip. "Is this clearly understood?"

"Yes," I said in terror, unloosening my hands. "Yes."

"For if it is not, you will be punished."

15

Visitors from the Mainland

With Don Enrique's threat ringing in my ears, I ran up the endless stairs. As I changed my clothes I saw six carriages, drawn by horses whose manes were decked with flowers, leave the harbor and start up the winding road toward the castle.

When I was dressed I went to warn Dorothy D'Amico. I found two Yaqui *pistoleros* standing stiffly against her door, their eyes fixed in a hard, Indian stare.

"I wish to pass," I said.

Their eyes remained blank. They would not move until Captain Vega gave the order, one of them said.

"Can you hear me?" I called to Dorothy. A faint voice answered but I was unable to make out the words. "There are guards at your door," I said.

"I know," she answered. "I've tried to leave. Yesterday I was invited to the party. That was yesterday. Today, one hour ago, Alicia came to the door with a gold bar and a choker of pearls."

She must have heard my gasp, even through the thick,

ironbanded door, and the short silence as I struggled for words.

"What should I do?" she said calmly, so calmly that it frightened me.

The *pistoleros* were listening, though they understood not a word of English.

"Nothing will happen until the party's over," I said. "There are double locks on the doors. Keep them locked. Whoever comes, don't let them in."

"Can Father Martínez help?"

"No."

"Christopher?"

"No one can help you except Don Enrique," I said. "The party has begun. I'll talk to him and come back."

I ran to the balustrade that looked down upon the terrace. A mariachi band was tuning up. Yaqui servants in huaraches and red ponchos were gliding about with crystal trays of fizzing lemonade and margaritas in wide-mouthed glasses frosted with salt. The *anglo* guests—there looked to be two dozen at least—were clustered around the barbecue pit where a row of wild boar had been steaming since morning, wrapped in burlap sacks and covered with a blanket of wet earth. In their midst, a head taller than any of the *gringos*, was Don Enrique.

I stood on the balcony until he looked up and saw me. There must have been something about me—my rigid body, my face that felt drained of blood—that held his attention. A spectral Ophelia saying, "Come, my coach! Good night. Good night. There's rosemary, that's for remembrance." Or silent, a threat upon my tongue. I did not move until he left the crowd and came toward me. I met him on the landing, halfway to the terrace.

"You looked terribly disturbed standing there on the balcony," he said. "All alone. Like an apparition. One of the *gringas* remarked on it, otherwise I would not have seen you." He took my arm in a firm grip. His fingers were long and thin, pale stalks. Their strength always surprised me.

"What disturbs you?" he said. "Have you had another vision of your mother? What is it?"

"It is Dorothy D'Amico. I have just talked to her. She was supposed to attend the party tonight. But guards are at her door and she can't leave."

"Why does that upset you?" my father said. "You know that she's been writing a book. She started the day she arrived. It's about the islands, the mines, Castillo Santiago, about me, even about you. An unfriendly book. Fortunately I learned about it in time."

"You've already destroyed what she has written. Why don't you let her leave the island?"

"Because she would begin on the book again as soon as she got to the mainland."

He tightened his grip on my arm and started down the steps toward the terrace. I pulled away from him.

"Remove the guards from her door," I said, "and let her go."

The band was playing now, but my voice rose above the sound. There was a threat in it that was not lost upon him. He glanced down at the crowd of *anglos*. Some were looking up at us. All of them must have been aware of the scene, heard my words. He was embarrassed and angry, fearful that I would say more, that in a moment I might shout some scandalous threat.

"I will speak to Captain Vega," he said, "and have the guards removed at once." He took my arm again. "Now come and meet our guests. And do not forget that we share secrets."

"There will be no secrets," I said, "if Dorothy D'Amico is not allowed to leave the island."

"She can leave when she wishes," he said.

I did not believe him.

I had already formed a picture of the *gringas* I would meet at the party, based upon the nineteen who had come to Isla del Oro. The picture was wrong completely.

Don Enrique had designed a fine-meshed net that, cast

112

upon the waters, had brought in a catch of women, all of them young, blonde and pretty, except for Dorothy D'Amico who was beautiful. These *gringas* were quite the opposite. Two were young and attractive. The rest were matronly.

Supper was waiting for us. The three fat boar were ready on a serving table, squatting on their haunches with ripe tuna apples in their mouths. The cook sliced off a piece of meat and handed it to Don Enrique who doused it in a mound of salt—he liked salt as much as he liked meat—tried it on his tongue, said it would be improved by two more hours of steaming, but nodded his approval.

Before I sat down to supper I ran back to the tower. The guards were still there. Through the door I told Dorothy that I had talked to Don Enrique and had a promise from him that the guards would be removed. Doubtful, she said nothing in reply.

The tables were set around the barbecue pit and decorated with sunbursts of little flags, the red and yellow flags of Spain. I ate with two *anglos*.

The woman was fat and wrapped in a voluminous sari. Her face was round and pink and looked jolly, but she had mean little eyes lurking beneath heavy eyebrows. America had become, she said, a gigantic bawdy house. Her intention was to sweep it clean with a stiff broom, made of fiery bristles. In this task she would be assisted by a thousand workers living in cells throughout the state of California. And by divine guardians, since she was, she said, a half-sister of Jesus. She held her knife and fork tightly in her plump, heavily ringed hands. As I listened to her she became Madame Defarge in *A Tale of Two Cities,* and the knife and fork turned into knitting needles as she sat on the eve of the French Revolution knitting down the names of those whom she wished to send to the guillotine.

Mr. Cranshaw sat across from me. He was a tall man, even when sitting down, with a bald head and sharp-pointed sideburns touched up with dye. He was a vice-president of F.F.F., the Federation for Family Freedom.

"Many believe," he said, "that when the nine hundred drank poison and died in Jonestown the Temple collapsed. But, Miss Señorita, the idea did not. Like Christ from the tomb, it is rising again. Not in Guiana. No, in the forests and mountains of California, where we have large stores of all the things that will be required."

After supper I excused myself and hurried off in search of Christopher. I located him at the far end of the terrace, talking to a woman draped in a silver shawl. Fog was rolling in from the sea, as it did every night now that spring was here, and I didn't learn until I was quite close that it was Gerda Wolfe.

When I turned around and started back, waiting for their conversation to end, a young man stepped in front of me. Attired in a black leather jacket with two zippered pockets, from one of which issued sounds similar to those I had heard from Jennifer Delaney's *gringo* records. He took out a lighter and a package of cigarettes and, after he had offered me one, lit one for himself with a long blue flame. In the blue light his face, which was small and wide-mouthed, had a menacing look. There was a thin scar on his cheek and a tattoo on the back of one of his hands.

"I am Alexander Carrboro," he said, and when I showed no sign of recognizing him he added, "You must have heard the name."

"I've heard of Alexander the Great," I said, jokingly.

"Your father knows it," he said, "or I would not be here."

"Should I know you?"

"No, you're too young."

"Who are you, Mr. Carrboro?" I said.

He hesitated, not sure, it seemed, quite where to start, or whether to start at all. The radio in his pocket was playing softly, over and over, the words "Too late, too late, I learned to hate.'' He hunched his shoulders and I thought he was about to walk away when he took a step closer.

"I like barbecue," he said. "An interesting party, but I have never met any of the guests before. Have you?"

I shook my head.

"Your father has an idea about freeing California from some of its idiocies," Mr. Carrboro said, turning off the radio. "He wants to send half the population back to where they came from and then reeducate the rest. Do you know anything about it?"

"He's never discussed such a thing with me," I said.

"It all sounds pretty vague from what little I've heard. Sort of an antiseptic, peaceful revolution. There's no such thing as a peaceful revolution. No more than there's a peaceful typhoon or a happy disaster. You break eggs to make a soufflé and heads to make a revolution.''

"Nietzsche observed that a revolution moves at the pace of a dove," I said.

"At first, maybe," Mr. Carrboro said.

Over his shoulder I kept watching Christopher and Gerda Wolfe. She was doing most of the talking, using her white hands in graceful gestures, elegantly tossing her head. She wore gold earrings shaped like stilettos that despite the fog caught the light from the myriad of lanterns strung overhead.

Mr. Carrboro was telling me about his childhood in Argentina—his father had been a member of the United States embassy there—and how he came to admire the Black September guerrillas and how he first became a guerrilla himself. I think he mentioned some group called the Weathermen.

"There are problems that can be solved in only one way," he said, now speaking fluent Spanish. "Only by violence. *Siempre la violencia!*"

He tossed his cigarette away as if he were tossing a bomb. It made a fiery arc in the night. His voice went on and on, describing horrors—people and parts of people lying on the ground, Khartoum, New York, Munich . . .

"It must be dangerous," I said, "being a revolutionary."

"It's dangerous now to walk down the street in broad daylight," Mr. Carrboro said. "They mug you for a postage stamp. Danger is everywhere."

"But apparently you go looking for it. What if you get caught and sent to prison for the rest of your life?"

"I'll not be caught." He took out a small silver box from his pants pocket and opened it. Inside was a crystalline tablet. "Cyanide," he said.

Cyanide was used at the smelter to extract gold from ore. He saw that I was puzzled.

"It kills you," he said. "A friend in need."

"Just one tablet?"

"In a minute. In less time than that."

Christopher came out of the fog and rescued me. As he walked away, Mr. Carrboro said, *"Hasta la vista.* Until then," and turned on the radio in his pocket.

The mariachi band was playing "Cielita Linda" and all the guests were dancing. As I started to tell Christopher about Dorothy D'Amico, he interrupted me.

"I've learned a few things from Gerda Wolfe. Bits of her past," he said. "She was born in Austria, went to school in Frankfurt, and was studying medicine when Hitler came to power. She says she hated everything he stood for. This I doubt. I think she was mixed up in some of his activities. And I am certain now that she is the one who killed the eighteen women and embalmed their bodies. Experimented on them before they were killed. Who else on the island has these skills? No one."

I stopped and stared at him. "Experimented?"

"I went back to the chamber again, last night after I finished work on the Serra project," Christopher said. "I told you that it had been postponed? Yes, well I found the doors open, both of them."

"Don Enrique's not trying to keep the place a secret," I said. "Not from me, at least. He told me so."

"Working on a very strong suspicion, I confirmed several things I had happened to notice before," Christopher said. "All of the women are wearing pearl collars. And at the lower edge of these collars, on both sides of the neck, there's a line, thin as gossamer. An attempt has been made to conceal them with paste."

"Incisions?"

"Yes, and several details about them interest me. They were made by a surgeon. No two are alike. The carotids supply blood to different parts of the head. You can put a person into a stupor by compressing one of these arteries. He will bleed to death in minutes if they are severed. These incisions were not meant to kill. They were experimental."

The music had ended. The *gringa* in the voluminous sari was coming toward us. Without a word I left Christopher and made my way through the crowd in search of my father. He was not on the terrace. I learned from Mercedes that he had gone to the castle and would return. Believing that he had gone to release Dorothy, as he had promised to do, I hurried to her rooms. The guards were still there, one on each side of the door, staring straight before them.

I ran to the library. The lamps were on, there were papers on his desk, but he was not there. As I was leaving, I heard steps. It was Villaverde, the neat little man who seldom smiled, my father's favorite.

He smiled now, a tight, barely visible movement of his lips. "May I be of help?" he said.

"Have you seen Don Enrique?"

"Yes, he was here a moment ago."

"Do you know where he went?"

"I believe to the chapel."

"Will you see? Please hurry."

He went off quickly, moving without a sound on his neat, rubber-soled shoes. In a short time he came back to say that

Don Enrique had been to the chapel, according to the old woman who minded the door, had lit candles and left.

"Do you wish me to search further?" said Villaverde. "He might have gone back to the terrace."

I was struck with a sudden thought. On an impulse I took the stairs that led downward to the pantheon, my breath tight in my throat.

16

Guardian of
the Gate

The first of the two doors was ajar. The second was closed but not locked. It swung heavily on its gold hinges, taking all of my strength. A gust of sweet incense enveloped me.

It was quiet except for the faintest of sounds, the flicker of a thousand flames. A wall of thin blue mist stood between the ceiling and the floor. Through it, toward the middle of the room, I made out a figure. It was my father. He was walking down the row of coffins, stopping at each one, peering through the crystal lids, making a courtly bow, and passing on.

At the last coffin, the nineteenth, the one intended for Dorothy D'Amico, he paused to touch his forehead and then his breast. He made the obeisance thoughtfully, as though God were watching him.

Distinctly I heard him say, quoting Blake, whom he often read, "To be cast out is part of God's design. The road of excess leads to the Palace of Wisdom."

It could have been a sound or a shadow cast upon the wall

that caught my attention. Or the way my father suddenly turned to glance at something behind him.

I left the doorway and started down the aisle between the wall and the row of caskets. In front of me I saw a moving shape. I heard a sound that leaves in a wind might make and realized that the shape was the serpent, the beautiful pink and black bushmaster.

The serpent was not in pursuit of Don Enrique, only following him, it seemed, its lidless gemlike eyes watchful like those of a true friend and guardian. It wound itself quite close to him and then stopped to arrange its shining coils and flick its tongue, ready to move if my father moved.

I said in the steadiest voice I could summon, "The serpent is following you."

Don Enrique must not have heard my voice nor known that I was there behind him, for he paid no heed to my warning and said in ringing tones, " 'Golden Spain, burst the barriers of old Rome! The fiery limbs, the flaming hair, shot like the sinking sun into the Western Sea.' "

He lowered his gaze and crossed himself once more. It was then, as he opened his eyes, that he saw me. A moment passed while he collected his thoughts.

"You, Lucinda," he said, surprised. "The incense and candle smoke curling about create singular shapes." His head moved forward and he fixed his eyes upon me. Surprise changed suddenly to anger. "You have followed me here to plead for your friend, D'Amico."

"Not to plead," I said, "but to warn you that unless you release her I will go and from the balcony announce to your guests that she is being held prisoner. Far worse. That Gerda Wolfe, who's there on the terrace, dancing daintily in her silver dress and gold earrings, will . . ."

"Traitoress!" he shouted.

He shouted the word twice more. He took a lurching step toward me and raised both fists. The serpent, which rested, waiting, not two paces away, now moved its coils.

Only a second or two passed between the shout and my

father's gestures, but in that brief time I recalled the words of the zoo keeper: "The bushmaster is reluctant to attack unless provoked."

The friendly serpent, feeling itself threatened by the angry words and the raised fists, moved noiselessly forward. In one graceful gathering of its great length, the tip of its tail resting upon the marble floor, the pink jaws stretched wide, it flung itself upon Don Enrique.

He raised his hands, but the serpent's sharp fangs struck his throat, and as he flinched and turned away, grasping at the writhing coils, it struck again, so quickly that the two strikes appeared to be one.

I believe that for a moment he did not feel the blows. But he must have heard my screams, for like a father who wishes to comfort a frightened child, he stretched his hands toward me.

He was borne backward and fell to his knees. He glanced at the serpent, marked in beautiful bands of pink and black, with almost a look of affection.

Slowly he said, "To be cast out is part of God's design . . ."

His voice faded to a whisper. He tried to rise and failed. The serpent rustled away among the caskets.

Kicking off my slippers, I ran out of the chamber and up the stairs to the balcony. I groped my way through the blinding mist, guided by the sound of music and laughter.

Three men came toward me from the direction of the terrace. I stepped aside to let them pass. The first man carried a lantern. I recognized him as Captain Vega. Close behind him came a *pistolero* armed with a sword, followed by Christopher Dawson.

Christopher recognized me at once. "Vega ordered my arrest," he said. "I was dancing with one of the guests, and he walked out on the floor and picked me up. I don't know where he's taking me."

In a few words I told him about Don Enrique. "I am on my way to tell Dr. Wolfe."

"She's on the terrace," he said. "After you tell her, get to the *Infanta*. Put in an SOS for the Coast Guard. There's someone on board who can place the call. Don't let Captain Wolfe know what you're doing."

Dr. Wolfe was dancing with Mr. Cranshaw. I ran up and explained what had happened. "He's in the chamber."

"What chamber?" she asked.

"The chamber," I said, "at the far end of the tunnel."

"What tunnel?" she said.

"The one that leads out of the crypt," I said. When she pretended never to have heard of it, I shouted, "You know where it is. You have been there, Dr. Wolfe!"

Her thick glasses looked green in the mist. Her pale blue eyes were hidden.

Two carriages stood in the driveway. I chose the one driven by Panchito, who had a long, braided whip with an iron tassel on the end and liked to use it. He shouted an Indian cry and we careened wildly toward the harbor.

I could barely see the *Infanta*. Her white side and upper deck were lost in the fog. Just her riding lights showed, high on the mast. A dim figure, a sailor, was sitting on the companionway that led to the bridge. Playing a guitar, he sang in a sad voice, *"Cu, cu, curu, paloma."* He was the same young man I had seen the morning I tried to leave the island. He was singing the same song.

"Are there officers aboard?" I said.

He got to his feet slowly. He didn't recognize me.

"I wish to call the Coast Guard."

He laid the guitar in the case tenderly, closed and fastened the lid, and put it under his arm, now humming the song.

"Please hurry," I said. "It's an emergency. Call an officer."

"No officers on this ship. They're up with the party," he said. "Someday I'll be an officer myself. Maybe sooner. It's Captain Wolfe who makes it hard on me. My name is Miguel Maximillano."

"The *teléfono*," I said.

122

"Sure," he said. *"Seguro que sí."*

He led me to the bridge. The radio-telephone was behind the wheel. He sat down and began to fiddle at the console. When all the red lights were glowing and a whining noise came from somewhere, he started over, trying each of the buttons and switches once more. After a long time—probably only a minute or less—he had the Coast Guard on the phone and I was telling an ensign about the accident.

"I hear you. Don't shout," the ensign said. "You're blasting me out of the shack. Where are you?"

"At the wharf on Isla del Oro. On board the *Infanta.*"

"Where am I?" he asked himself. There was a short silence. "Cruising about twenty-six miles away. The E.T.A. for Isla del Oro is . . . twelve thirty-six."

I asked him what E.T.A. meant.

"Estimated time of arrival."

"How long would it take the *Infanta* to reach the mainland?"

"I know the ship. In weather like tonight, with the fog, one hour and twenty minutes," he said.

The ship's clock above my head showed 11:51. The phone was silent and I thought it had gone dead. Then the ensign was talking again.

"I've been in touch with *Buenaventura,*" he said. "She's ten minutes closer than we are. She's on her way."

"Will she have anti-venom?" I said.

"For what?"

"For a bushmaster."

"I doubt it."

The phone went dead. I climbed down from the bridge. Miguel was on the deck with his guitar under his arm, humming *"Cu, cu, curu"* again.

I groped my way to the gangplank and stood there peering shoreward, I was afraid to go farther, lest I lose myself in the fog. The castle lights no longer showed.

Four men came out of the gray night bearing a stretcher, Gerda Wolfe walking on one side, Christopher and Father

Martínez on the other. As they passed I caught a glimpse of my father, his face swollen to twice its size.

They took Don Enrique into the main salon and placed him on a couch. I went over and put my hand on his forehead. It was cold with sweat that had dried on his skin.

"We must take him to the mainland," Dr. Wolfe said to me. "I haven't the required drugs."

Foolishly, I remembered the helicopter that once had landed on the island, that Don Enrique still held. It was sitting in a shed less than a mile from the ship. I asked Father Martínez about it.

"I can't fly the thing," he said. "And there's no one on the island who can. And it can't fly itself."

"A Coast Guard ship will be here in fifteen minutes," I said to Gerda Wolfe. "I've talked to them."

"A Coast Guard ship," Gerda Wolfe said, "is not a hospital. Don Enrique requires the best of care. This can be found on the mainland only."

She stood in the middle of the room, her pale blue eyes fixed upon me.

"I repeat," she said. Her voice rose. "Don Enrique must have hospital care."

She glanced at Captain Wolfe, a silent command to start the engines. The thought struck me that once out of the harbor, the ship would never reach the mainland, never return to Isla del Oro.

"A Coast Guard ship will be here in fifteen minutes," I repeated.

Dr. Wolfe gathered her thin lips into a smirk. "The Coast Guard is not reliable. We had an emergency here a year ago. You will remember. An explosion. We expected help from them early in the morning. They showed up at noon."

She took a gliding step toward me. Her face was flushed with anger. "This is a matter of life and death," she said. "I am his doctor. It is my decision."

"And I am his daughter," I said. "I wish to keep him here."

The cabin was quiet. The only sound I was aware of was my father's breathing. One moment it sounded loud, then it was gentle, then it seemed as though he wasn't breathing at all.

Dr. Wolfe was still wearing her silvery-gray party dress, and her pendant earrings that looked like stilettos. In the light of the gimbal lamps the earrings changed shape. Suddenly they were two sharp scalpels, and I saw her standing in a white gown before a white table in a white room. I saw her reach up and take one of the shining knives . . .

There was a far-off whisper, the faintest of sounds, scarcely that, more of an airy movement, as if something had left the room.

Father Martínez was holding Don Enrique's hand. He turned to me. "Your father," he said in a quiet voice, "is dead."

Dr. Wolfe made a curious sound in her throat. "He can't be!" she cried. She went to the couch and felt for my father's pulse. "His heart beats," she said, facing me. "It beats faintly, but it beats."

Christopher shook his head. His lips did not move, but plainer than spoken words he said to me what was already in my thoughts: This woman is lying. Don Enrique is dead.

An officer was standing at the doorway. Dr. Wolfe must have given him a signal, for he disappeared at once. The big engines started up, there was a long blast from the ship's horn, and the *Infanta* moved from the wharf.

I ran out of the cabin shouting. Men were working on the wharf, but they did not answer. Helplessly, I watched them fade away in the fog.

I could see no farther than the bow of the ship. Above me the radar moved in a circle, scanning the harbor. The ship's bell rang without stopping and every few seconds there was a long, angry blast from the *Infanta's* horn.

We were lost in a world of driving mist and frightening sounds. From far off, between the roars of the horn, louder than the ringing of the bell, I heard the sound of a second horn.

At the same moment I made out the two tall rocks that guard the harbor from the sea. The hazy rays of a searchlight loomed through the fog. Our engines slowed. The ship moved ever so cautiously for a short time, then suddenly stopped and began to move astern.

The searchlight that now fell squarely across our bow belonged to the cutter *Buenaventura*. Since there wasn't seaway enough for us both to pass in the Narrows, and the cutter was already upon us, it occurred to me that Captain Wolfe had decided to wait until she sailed through and then make a run for the open sea.

17

Cu, Cu, Curu, Paloma

The Buenaventura *came* silently out of the fog, so near that I could read her name, then so close that I could see a sailor at her rail. He called a greeting through cupped hands and I returned it. The ships were now side by side.

"This is the *Infanta*," I shouted. "We have trouble on board. In God's name, please help us!"

A dory pulled alongside the *Infanta*. An officer, muffled against the raw night, climbed the ladder and stepped out on deck. He introduced himself as Lieutenant Murdock.

"Are you the one who did the shouting?" he said.

"Yes," I said in a trembling voice.

Gerda Wolfe was waiting. She stood beside my father, her feet wide apart and her hands on her hips, as though she had been protecting him from harm and would continue to do so. Only a thin, red crease between her brows betrayed her fear.

"The man who lies on the couch behind me," she said, "is Don Enrique de Cabrillo y Benivides."

Lieutenant Murdock glanced down at the swollen body.

Even in its gruesome state he recognized it as the body of the man who had ruled Isla del Oro, who had treated him with lordly disdain, a man whom over the years he had come to fear. Even in death, my father seemed to cast a spell upon him, for the officer stood there speechless.

"Don Enrique was bitten by a poisonous snake," Gerda Wolfe was saying. "He died only a few moments ago. I am now taking him to the mainland to report the . . ."

The lieutenant roused himself. "You're a nurse?" he said.

"I am Dr. Wolfe," she said stiffly.

"I have heard of you," the officer said. "You are the resident doctor on Isla del Oro."

Dr. Wolfe nodded. A moment later Captain Wolfe came in briskly with four members of the crew and carried the body away.

"With your permission," he said to the officer, "I will continue our voyage to the mainland."

"Why not?" Lieutenant Murdock said absent-mindedly. He had gray hair and blue eyes. He spoke slowly and wore horn-rimmed glasses, but he seemed not to be very bright. "Why not?" he said again.

Captain Wolfe hurried out of the cabin. I heard him running along the passage that led to the ship's bridge. There was a blast from the *Infanta*. A second blast.

"Mother Mary in Heaven," I prayed. "Don't let them escape!" Then I realized that the ship couldn't move until the *Buenaventura* pulled out of the Narrows. I kept on praying anyway, saying the words to myself.

Lieutenant Murdock glanced at me. I believe he had forgotten that I stood not more than six feet away.

"The dead man we have accounted for," he said, speaking the words a Wilkie Collins detective might have used. "Is there anything else?"

"A murderess," I said.

"Murderess?" he repeated, removing his glasses and wiping off the mist with his handkerchief.

It struck me from the surprised way he spoke that he thought murders were only committed by men, that he had never heard of Lady Macbeth or fabled Clytemnestra.

Dr. Wolfe walked to the doorway and peered out through the fog at the ship that now lay broadside to us, blocking the passage.

"The murderess," Lieutenant Murdock said, studying me over the top of his glasses to make sure that he was not talking to a hysterical female.

Dr. Wolfe turned quickly and spoke to him. "Don Enrique's death has been a great shock," she said in a flat, emotionless voice. "It has been a dreadful, dreadful day. I hope you will pardon me if I retire?"

Without waiting for a reply, she left the cabin. She did not take the stairs to the sleeping quarters. Instead, she went up the passageway to the ship's bridge, the same one Captain Wolfe had taken moments before.

"The murderess," I said, "has just left the cabin."

Lieutenant Murdock squinted. "You mean the doctor?"

"Dr. Wolfe," I said. I waited until he fully grasped the name. "She's the murderess and she's gone to warn her husband . . ."

"About what?"

"That you are ready to seize the ship."

"Seize the ship? I don't understand."

"There are eighteen women up there in the castle," I said, pointing. "They're all dead."

I scarcely expected Lieutenant Murdock would believe me. He didn't. He started to clean his glasses again, changed his mind, and put them back on. His mouth fell open. He shut it and with a grim effort kept it shut.

There was a short silence. Seeking, I presumed, some word of sanity, he turned to Father Martínez.

Before the father could answer, I said, "Eighteen dead women are hidden in the castle. We think that Dr. Wolfe killed them."

"You think?" the lieutenant broke in. He removed his coat and laid it on a chair. "Who owns the ship?" he said.

"This girl," Christopher said. "Lucinda de Benivides."

The big engines were quiet. Only the faintest vibration beneath my feet told me they were running. Bells, one after the other, sounded deep in the ship and the engines speeded up.

A moment later Captain Wolfe came down the passageway and stopped at the door that opened into the cabin. With a slow glance he surveyed Lieutenant Murdock and the rest of us. In each hand he held a long-barreled pistol. Gerda Wolfe stood behind him..

"Lieutenant," he said, "your ship is blocking my path. I request you to move her. By the rules of the sea, I have the right of passage."

"The rights of passage," Lieutenant Murdock said, "are suspended until further notice."

"I am moving through," Captain Wolfe said, raising the pistols to his chest.

The cutter *Buenaventura* was half the size of the *Infanta*, not more than seventy feet in length, and not nearly so fast. The *Infanta* could shunt her aside and outdistance her to Mexican waters, out of reach of the Coast Guard and all United States authorities.

Captain Wolfe spoke one word to a sailor who stood at his side. With this signal, three sailors quietly set upon Lieutenant Murdock, forced a gag in his mouth, and wrestled him to the boards.

Gerda Wolfe looked at me, her glasses flashing in the light of the gimbal lamp. She looked at her husband and nodded. Believing that this was another signal, a signal to tie me up, I backed away toward the door.

The *Buenaventura* still lay alongside, only the bumpers holding us apart. The *Infanta*'s searchlight swept the Narrows. The engines had settled down to a steady purr. From the bridge, someone shouted a command.

The gentle words of a love song came from the passage at

my back. I was about to shout a warning to the *Buenaventura*. I don't know why I turned. In the passage, not two paces behind Captain Wolfe, stood Miguel Maximillano. He held his guitar in one hand and a hunting rifle in the other. He grinned and waved the rifle from side to side, humming to himself.

He fired only one shot. But in the heavy silence that had fallen upon us it sounded like a bomb. The bullet went through the patent-leather beak on Captain Wolfe's cap and struck the panel behind him.

Miguel was about to fire once more, then he decided not to. He dropped the rifle and casually disappeared, humming *"Cu, cu, curu, paloma . . ."*

18

The Wolfes

The day after the deaths of Captain Wolfe and Don Enrique, the mainland descended upon Isla del Oro.

They came by rubberneck steamers, aboard sailboats and fancy cruisers, even in flimsy skiffs powered by outboard motors. They anchored off the Narrows and snapped pictures of Castillo Santiago. They came by airplane and helicopter, clouding the skies. But of the thousands of sightseers that gathered near the island, only one ventured ashore. Someone evaded our guards (he must have swum underwater from a ship), landed in the cove with a camera, climbed the steep cliff to the terrace and hid himself in the shrubbery. I didn't know the intruder had been there until I was shown a newspaper printed in Los Angeles—the first newspaper I had ever seen.

There was I, staring out from the first page, gawking at something or other, the wind blowing my hair in all directions. Dressed in a jumpsuit I had carelessly put on that morning, I looked fat and distressed. Below the picture were these misleading words:

"Beautiful Lucinda de Cabrillo y Benivides, heiress of billionaire monarch of island where the bodies of eighteen women were discovered . . ."

The picture astounded me. I looked more like a scullery maid than an heiress. I was even more astounded by the newspaper itself.

I bit my lips, remembering that only a few short days ago newspapers were forbidden on Isla del Oro. I was still committing a forbidden act. I felt like an explorer who comes upon a buried tomb and pauses there in fear of an ancient curse inscribed upon the doorway—"Beware all those who would enter here."

I read the stories beside my picture and below it, or rather the lines in black type: "County official indicted for fraud"; "Engineer and girl friend killed in crash"; "Mother and three children burn in arson fire"; "Millions stolen from armored truck"; "Four hundred guerrillas die in San Salvador rout."

I turned the page, to a picture of twenty-one cars piled up in a fog, to an old woman mugged by teenagers, lying in a hospital bed, her head wrapped in bandages, seriously wounded but expected to live. Someone was suing and being sued. I reached a page where men were kicking a ball with all the excitement of children, and others were punching each other in the face. I closed the newspaper. My hands were gray from the ink that had come from its pages.

In the past, standing at my window, I had often tried to imagine the world beyond Isla del Oro. It was no more to me than a wavy line on the horizon—when you could see it— blue sometimes, an amber glow in the dark and the shifting beam of a lighthouse.

A shudder of fear ran through me at the world I had just encountered. I crossed the room and threw the paper in the fire and watched while it was consumed.

The coroner and his assistants came from the mainland, along with a band of detectives, my father's lawyer, Don

Anselmo de Alicantera, two secretaries, and Don Anselmo's son, Justino.

The detectives collected statements from Father Martínez and Captain Vega, from me and Dorothy D'Amico, from everyone including the twenty-nine servants. When they left they took with them Miguel, the boy who owned the high-powered rifle and played sad little songs on his guitar. He swore, even when the detectives called him a liar, that he had shot Captain Wolfe because the captain had told him to throw his guitar into the bay and to try something more suited to his talents, like a bongo drum. Besides, if Captain Wolfe stole the ship, as he was sure the captain planned to do, he would never see Isla del Oro again.

They also took with them Gerda Wolfe, bound in manacles, her lips sealed in stony silence, her eyes blank behind her thick glasses.

After a day in the crystal chamber, Coroner Frye reported that two of the women had died from cyanide poisoning—he surmised that the others had died in the same way—and that, in his words, "all were the objects of complicated medical experimentation."

His assistants gathered up the coffins, the bones of Juan Rodqiguez Cabrillo, and the Nayarit Indian. As he left on the cutter *Buenaventura,* the coroner offered to send me a copy of the official autopsies if I wished to see them, which I didn't.

The lawyers stayed on. There were important matters to decide. For one thing, the problem of inheritance. I was a minor, not yet eighteen. A guardian must be appointed. Other problems worried Don Anselmo de Alicantera.

"There's a good chance," he said, "even a probability, of damage suits filed by relatives of the eighteen women or those who claim to be relatives. You will remember Howard Hughes."

I didn't. I never had heard of Howard Hughes.

"Anyway," Don Anselmo continued, perplexed at my ignorance, "this young man who ran a gas station in the

Mojave Desert showed up in court with a piece of paper that he claimed was Hughes's will, which Hughes had dropped by one day and just handed to him.''

"It happens a lot of the time," his son Justino said. "You never know how many relatives you have until you die.''

The weather was beautiful—the velo clouds held off. The lawyers and stenographers remained for three days. They worked in the mornings. In the afternoons they swam in the cove's frigid waters and nursed themselves back to life on the bright terrace, with the warm sun and Castillo Santiago's excellent wines.

Don Anselmo was really concerned about my future, worried over everything—the responsibilities connected with the mines, the castle, which was overstaffed with servants waiting to steal me blind, the flock of salesmen making ready to descend upon me, the droves of fortune-hunters, my health, my education, everything. My education especially.

"Have you given thought to college?" he asked. Before I could answer, he said, "My daughter is in her first year at Stanford. It's a hard university to get into, but if you apply now, take time to bone up, you can pass the regents' examination, I'm sure.''

Regents' examination! The words, whatever they meant, had an ominous sound.

Justino spoke up and rattled off a long list of other colleges where I could go for an education. The names ran together in one big blur.

Justino was tall, with tawny skin, and black Spanish hair that curled and came together in a tangled ducktail at the back of his neck.

But I didn't see him as doomed and driven Heathcliff, striding across the stormy moor to declare undying love for Cathy Earnshaw. Instead, he was a young man sitting on a bench, dressed in Levi's and a short-sleeved, pure-cotton shirt.

I sat and said little and watched the ships cruising along

the shore, a helicopter hovering overhead, the sun afloat on the western sea. I hoped that nothing would happen to keep the Alicanteras on the island for another day. The gray stone wall in my mother's bedroom was a cold blade aimed at my heart.

Don Anselmo and his son did remain another day. We had gone through two of Don Enrique's mammoth safes the afternoon he arrived, but we couldn't find the combination of the third safe, so a locksmith was flown in from the mainland.

Don Anselmo's hope was that we would find a will, one written before or after the will Don Enrique had burned. We found neither, but we did come upon a manila envelope sealed with wax.

In the envelope were rough sketches for the building of the *Infanta* in Rota, Spain, suggestions for my parents' sleeping quarters—whether they should be located amidships or nearer the bow, away from the noise of the engines.

Curiously, among these sketches I found three letters from Captain Wolfe to my father. Curious because they had nothing to do with the construction of the *Infanta*.

Two of the letters were written from Paris to my father in Madrid and dated June 21 and July 3, 1973.

The first letter spoke of a previous meeting at Vilvoord, Belgium, during which my father had given Captain Wolfe a large sum to be used in payment of a debt.

The second letter, the one written two weeks later, asked for additional funds. Wolfe and his wife had reached Paris, but were in hourly danger of arrest by Kaspar Lenz.

The third letter, sent to Isla del Oro, was brief. Captain Wolfe and his wife had escaped from Paris and, after hiding for a month on the Spanish border, were now in Rota aboard the *Infanta*, undyingly grateful and at Don Enrique's command.

I puzzled over the letters. "Wolfe was the man killed on the *Infanta*," I told Don Anselmo. "His wife is the woman they arrested and took to the mainland. One or the other or both of them committed a crime somewhere in Europe. They were pursued by someone called Kaspar Lenz and my father helped them to escape. What do you think?''

''Well,'' Don Anselmo said, ''Kaspar Lenz is a West German Nazi hunter. His name has been in the newspaper lately, linked with the famous Nazi hunters Wiesenthal and Klarsfeld. Years ago he had something to do with the trial of Adolf Eichmann. If Kaspar Lenz is a Nazi hunter and if he is hunting for the Wolfes, then the Wolfes are Nazi criminals.''

It was that simple. It explained why for eight years and more Heinrich and Gerda Wolfe had slavishly taken orders from my father.

Don Enrique had met them somewhere soon after my mother had disappeared. He learned that they were fugitives, fleeing prosecution by the West German government. They happened to fit into the madness that had come upon him, so nicely that he made it possible for them to escape their pursuers and find a hiding place on Isla del Oro.

Don Anselmo and his son left that night by floatplane, but not before they had convinced me that electricity and the telephone should be brought to the island. And that I should have a newspaper to read, one every day, at least.

I was delighted to see their plane rumble across the harbor and soar away.

I watched until it was lost in the glow of mainland lights. Then I decided how best to tear down the gray stone wall that my father had built in a jealous rage, exhorting the workmen through the long hours, shouting threats and imprecations.

Before I went to sleep that night, still thinking of the stone wall and what might lie behind it, I heard a thrushlike sound like water falling from the mossy edge of a rock into a quiet pool. I jumped up and went to the window. On the ledge sat a bird so beautiful that it could only be the quetzal. I crept back to bed and listened. The quetzal sang most of the night, and when it stopped I dreamed that I was in a forest and still heard it singing.

When I told Dorothy about the quetzal, she said she had heard it too, and that it was a good omen.

19

Behind the Wall

Three of us—Dorothy, Christopher, and I—spent the next evening arguing about the best way to remove the wall. Christopher had spent half of his life taking walls down stone by stone, carefully storing the stones away, numbering them in some cases. He suggested that we follow the same plan.

"This is slow," I said. "There are expert *dinamiteros* on the island. They can remove it in minutes."

"The wall's at least two feet thick," Christopher said. "It will require a heavy charge of powder. Do you want the whole place wrecked? The sightseers cruising up and down the shore would hear a mysterious roar issue from Castillo Santiago and the newspapers would report that an explosion had rocked the island."

Dorothy favored my plan, I think because it promised a more dramatic turn to the story she was feverishly writing, now that her days on Isla del Oro were numbered.

However, by the time we parted I had decided to follow Christopher's advice. We would have one of the miners make a small breach in the wall. Christopher would then take over the task and finish it quietly, in his methodical way. But no sooner was I back in my tower, lying in bed and trying hard to fall asleep, than nagging thoughts overcame me. The servants in the castle and the people in the village had forgotten about John Wesley Blake. Should anything be done that would start tongues to wagging again and, now that the outside world had discovered Isla del Oro, bring us another flood of sightseers?

Yet, the long, cold blade of doubt still pointed at my heart. I could not rest another day until I knew for certain whether my mother lay behind the wall. At dawn, before the first shift left for the mines, I sent Mercedes to the village. She brought me Fernando, a grizzled *dinamitero* who had been on the island since boyhood and knew that loose talk was punished and silence rewarded.

Dorothy was so absorbed in her writing when we came in that she only glanced up and went back to work. I showed Fernando the gray stone wall.

"I want a hole in it big enough to crawl through" I told him. "But no big noise."

"The wall is thick?" he asked.

"Like this," I said from memory, stretching my arms wide.

"Too thick," the *dinamitero* said. "Too big for drill. Behind?"

"A clothes press. A closet," I said. "It's as wide as the wall. Two doors in front. I don't want them blown to pieces."

"We try," Fernando said.

He took a handful of powder from his bag, mixed some mud—common dirt and water—and made a plaster, which he set against the wall.

"Leave," he said.

Christopher had not appeared and I didn't wait. Dorothy stopped writing. We closed the door and stood behind it. I heard the *dinamitero* swear, bite off the end of a fuse, swear again. Then I heard a thud, soft as the sound of a book falling from a shelf, almost.

The *dinamitero* opened the door. *"Hola!"* he said, pointing at the hole he had made.

I took up a candle and walked through a cloud of sulfurous smoke to the wall. At its center was a jagged place scarcely large enough for my body. I gave him the candle, squeezed myself through the hole, and he handed it back.

Pieces of stone littered the alcove floor, but the massive doors stood untouched. I grasped hold of one of the gold knobs. Stiff from the long years of disuse, it would not turn.

Dorothy shouted something that I couldn't make out. I put the candle down so I could use both my hands. As the knob turned, there suddenly came to my mind scenes from a story by Honoré de Balzac called *La Grande Bretèche*. I unloosed the knob and stepped away.

Next to Cervantes and Unamuno, Balzac had been Don Enrique's favorite author, and this his favorite story among all that Balzac wrote. He had given it to me on my twelfth birthday.

As I stood there in the half-darkness, the candle guttering on the floor and Dorothy asking through the wall if I needed help, I understood for the first time why the story had fascinated him and why he had given it to me.

Monsieur de Merret, Balzac's hero, is jealous of his wife Josephine. Upon entering her bedroom one evening, he is certain that he hears a closet door click shut and bluntly asks her who is in the closet. She replies, "No one is in the closet." He asks her then to swear on a Spanish crucifix that the closet is empty, which she calmly does.

Whereupon Monsieur de Merret calls in the village mason, has the closet bricked up, and sits down to enjoy his wife's discomfort. He sits for twenty days. During the first days when noises come from the closet, whenever she implores him to release the dying man, he smiles and says, "You have sworn on the Cross that there is no one there."

Yes, Don Enrique had undoubtedly read Balzac's story before he walled up my mother's closet.

I took hold of the gold knob again. The door creaked open. The smell of a perfume my mother used, musty and overly sweet, assailed me.

I raised the candle and peered down the long row of suits and dresses. They were in perfect order, just as she had left them. Her many shoes also.

Shielding the light, I stumbled to the far end, where her coats hung. As I returned I saw Dorothy's eyes staring at me through the opening.

"What did you find?" she whispered.

"Nothing," I said. "It's empty."

"Empty?"

I crawled through the jagged hole. Dorothy was standing in the rubble holding a lamp toward me, wisps of black smoke curling around her.

"Empty," I said.

"How *could* it be?"

"Because Don Enrique was horribly mistaken. There was never anyone hiding in the room. He just imagined there was. He heard sounds, someone moaning. He wanted to. In a jealous rage, he imagined all of it."

20

Journey to a Strange Land

In my life on Isla del Oro, in all that time, I hadn't received a letter from the outside world except from Porfirio Puertoblanca in Madrid. All the letters sent to me, as I have said, were destroyed on my father's orders as soon as they reached the *Infanta*. Since his death letters had poured in.

They came by the hundreds from people I didn't know, wishing me well, hoping that I would never follow the paths of other rich girls like Barbara Hutton and Patty Hearst, whose names I had never heard. They came from libraries and schools and foundations asking for donations. From brokers with property to sell, like islands in the South Pacific and hotels in the West Indies.

However, of the dozens of letters delivered each day from the mainland, no word came from my mother. Don Anselmo had reasons for this.

"She may have sent letters to you in the past," he wrote, "and received no answer, unaware that Don Enrique destroyed all your mail. She may not know that he is dead."

Don Anselmo ended his letter by promising to find her,

wherever she was. Days later I got word from him that she had been traced from Panama City to Aruba and that a further report would follow. In the same letter he enclosed a list of things I should do and not do. Since he now was my legal guardian, I thought it best to pay heed to his suggestions. Indeed, I had no other choice.

I was to see that Captain Vega and his *pistoleros* did not interfere with the lighthouse planned for Punta Encantador on the northern tip of the island. Don Enrique had always opposed the project. He liked the sound of the buoys when winter storms set them in motion. But the idea of a light flashing through the darkness, every night in fair weather or foul, like an alien eye, enraged him. Thinking of two ships that had fatefully gone aground on Encantador, I was determined to see that the lighthouse was built.

I must extend every courtesy to the tax collector, which I did by showing him through the castle and around the island. (When he went back to the mainland, he sent us a statement that doubled our taxes.)

I was also to be courteous to the mining inspectors. They came, inspected our operations, from the digging of ore to the smelting of gold bars, and announced that we must either install electricity in the mines or shut them down. Barges piled high with machinery suddenly appeared from the mainland.

Since the mines were to have electricity and the miners would no longer have to climb out of the shafts with ore on their backs, I decided to have it brought to the castle, too. Word that soon they wouldn't need to trim candles and fill lamps, sweep with brooms, heat water, and cook with wood caused a celebration among the servants that lasted for two days and two nights.

Both Christopher and Dorothy were thoughtful friends. They couldn't do enough for me. But I felt that beneath their kindness was a sense of duty.

While searching on San Miguel Island for the remains of Juan Cabrillo, Christopher had discovered a fossil the size of an average dog, which belonged, he believed, to a pygmy elephant. To further this venture, I had him taken to the site aboard the *Infanta* and put ashore with enough supplies to last him a year.

Dorothy, who had almost finished her book on Isla del Oro, kept wishing for more information about the Spanish voyages of exploration than she could find in Don Enrique's library. So I sent her off—with the gold bar and the pearl necklace he had given her—to the *Archivo de Indias* in Seville.

Two weeks later, I received word from Don Anselmo that Francesca de Benivides was living in the West Indies on the island of St. Thomas. "She is married to John Wesley Blake," he wrote, "and is the mother of two girls, five and seven. Blake travels from island to island doing portraits of American tourists. After reading these reports, I gather that your mother is happy. She'll hear of Don Enrique's death, if she hasn't heard already. My advice is to wait for her to write you."

I was deeply relieved to receive this news. And curious about the two sisters I had suddenly acquired. What did they look like? Were they blondes or brunettes? Would they like me, would I like them? Curiously, too, I felt a funny twinge of jealousy now that they would come first in my mother's affection.

A few days later Don Anselmo wrote, "You must realize that in a short time, in less than two years, you will inherit Isla del Oro, its mines and many properties scattered throughout Mexico and South America. This will place a heavy burden upon your young shoulders. You must prepare yourself. I harbor the impression that you have given little thought to this great responsibility.

"Don Enrique, God rest and protect his troubled soul, lived in a world that now, with his death, no longer exists. You, my dear Lucinda, will live in a vastly different world, one of your own choosing, I trust."

Don Anselmo closed his letter with a long postcript.

"I suggest that you leave the island for a month or two and travel to Spain, where you have relatives and friends, perhaps to Italy, which you know from your reading. Dorothy D'Amico would make an ideal companion—or Mercedes, who seems to be your closest friend. Do make plans to go somewhere. You have been under great stress. There is much for you to forget. Travel serves that purpose well, better than anything I know. My wife and I would like to have you for a week or so before you leave on your travels. It will serve as a quiet introduction, so to speak, to a world that must be a mystery to you now and perhaps a little frightening."

Frightening? What a feeble description of how I felt. The mere thought of leaving Isla del Oro, just the physical act of leaving, frightened me. But to cross the channel, remembering all that I had read in the newspaper I had burned, was more than frightening. It was terrifying!

I read Don Anselmo's letter twice and put it away and didn't think about it again for days, though once I dreamed about leaving Isla del Oro. I sailed away, not on the *Infanta* but on a Spanish caravel. I had a huge cabin in the stern with windows on every side. But there was only a vast ocean to see, and the ship traveled for a thousand leagues and never hailed a single port.

At dawn I went to the chapel, prayed and made a brief confession to Father Martínez. I said nothing to him about the disturbing dream in which I was the lone passenger on a ship that sailed endlessly on a landless sea. Afterwards he was strolling along the cliff and I overtook him and gave him Don Anselmo's letter.

He read it through quickly and gave it back. I had the impression that he already knew what was in it.

"You've been wondering for years what was over there," he said, glancing toward the distant mainland. "It's time to find out. Don Anselmo is right. I agree with him. Go!"

146

He stopped on the path to pick a flower and place it in the buttonhole of his shabby cassock.

"But before you go," he said, "I can use some of the electricity we now have in the castle. I am getting too old to crank the dome open and shut by hand. You'll see to it? And another thing. Don Enrique was a hoarder of candle wax. A miser. At his request the dollops left over from hundreds of candles were carefully collected each morning, as you know, by Catalina and Carmen, melted down and made into new candles. They are not artists, this pair. Dear people, mother and daughter, but makers of wax monsters. The altar candles are a disgrace. In Guadalajara there's an artist, Juan Moreno. Do I have your permission to engage him? Excellent. I shall."

"And while you're at it, Father, you might also engage a tailor. You look very much like a mendicant. All you need to complete the picture is a battered tin cup."

"Among all this splendor," he said, taking in with a slow sweep of his hand the castle and its crenelated towers, the terraces and colonnades and gardens, "I am more comfortable in this threadbare condition."

He squinted toward the mainland where against the horizon—a rare sight even on a clear day—rose the silver dome that housed the giant telescope at Mount Palomar.

"When you go to the mainland, you might order me one of those seeing eyes, not necessarily so big, but . . ."

"What makes you think I am going to the mainland, Father Martínez?"

He opened his breviary and noisily closed it, made a clucking noise in his throat, a certain sign that he was on the verge of anger.

"Your father lived the past," he said. "You can't possibly wish to do the same. But if you could, you wouldn't find it all so wonderful. While Michelangelo was painting the Sistine and Donatello did his little David in a beribboned straw hat and the Duomo doors were carved in gold, the country was a stew of hostile cities where princes lived by killing each other, and every man—butcher and baker alike—had a dagger in his belt or else one in his gizzard. In those days most of the babies died before they became children, women were worn out at thirty from work and child-bearing, men were old at forty."

He opened his breviary and searched for a proper verse to illustrate his sermon. Finding none, he snapped it shut again.

"Your ideas," he said, "about the battered world we precariously cling to have come mostly from your father. From books written a hundred years ago or more. From the handful of *gringas* who came to the island. And also from one newspaper you happened to read in which the world's scum, barbarity, and violence were displayed in flaming colors. There are millions of people, rich and poor, who don't belong to that shoddy world. Who marry and live wholesome lives and raise children who have respect for themselves and for those less endowed, who, thanks to God, never appear in the headlines."

Once more he leafed through his breviary, muttered a Latin phrase which escaped me, and continued with his sermon as we toiled up the steep path in the hot sun.

"The Devil dogged your father's footsteps," he said. "The Devil whispered strange things in his ears. Sometimes I think he whispers strange things in yours. Take the matter of the Murillo portrait. I know that you had it stored away. Why?"

"Because I don't like it, is why."

"It's a portrait by a great artist of a beautiful girl."

"An unlucky girl, fated to live an unhappy life and a short one."

"What does her life have to do with yours, pray tell?"

I hesitated. "It's hard to explain."

"Hard because it can't be explained. It's childish. You're too old for such nonsense."

We had come to the edge of the cliff and the half circle of iron benches that looked out upon the sea. Father Martínez sat down to catch his breath, pulling his gown up to expose his thin shanks to the breeze.

Gulls were gliding over our heads, not moving their wings. In the waves below us otter were sunning themselves. Close to shore a whale and her baby were swimming northward side by side. I had watched this scene many times before. I knew that the mother had traveled from the frigid waters of Alaska southward thousands of miles to the warm waters of Mexico to bear her young. And that now, having given birth, she was returning.

I watched the pair until they swam out of sight. Then I left Father Martínez to his reading and went down the hill to the storeroom—Mercedes called it her Hell-hole—where she had put Teresa's portrait, carefully dusted it off, carried it up to the music room, hung it above the harpsichord on the hooks that had never been taken down, and opened the heavy drapes.

In the bright morning sun that poured through the window Teresa's portrait looked different. Her eyes were still blue-gray and silver. And as I stood there they still sought me out. Yet in their depths, as though many curtains had been withdrawn, I no longer saw a girl bereft. It was a woman who gazed down upon me now, her lips parted in a smile that said, "This life is mine, not yours, Lucinda de Cabrillo y Benivides. Go and live your own life. And whatever you do and whatever you find there, smile as I am smiling now."

About the Author

Scott O'Dell was a Newbery Medalist, a three-time Newbery Honor Book winner, a two-time winner of the German "Jugenbuchpreis", winner of the deGrummond and Regina medals, and a recipient of the Hans Christian Andersen Author Medal, the highest international recognition for a body of work by an author of children's books.

Other Scott O'Dell books for Fawcett Juniper are ALEXANDRA, THE CASTLE IN THE SEA, THE ROAD TO DAMIETTA, STREAMS TO THE RIVER, RIVER TO THE SEA, and THE SERPENT NEVER SLEEPS.

Mr. O'Dell died in 1989.